THE SPIDER:
DICTATOR OF THE DAMNED

MASTER OF MEN!

DICTATOR OF THE DAMNED

By Grant Stockbridge

STEEGER BOOKS • 2020

CHAPTER 1
THE CALL TO DOOM

YOUNG FRANK DUNNING was visibly nervous as he tooled the long limousine expertly in to the curb before his employer's residence on Madison Avenue. He threw a quick glance over his shoulder, as if fearing the quick, deadly burst of a submachine gun from somewhere in the obscurity of the shadows across the street.

He slid swiftly out from behind the wheel, and held the door open for the Honorable Howard Appleton to alight. At the same time he carefully scanned the pedestrians who were passing. The Honorable Howard Appleton dismissed him and hurried up the steps of the old brownstone residence.

Frank Dunning, eyeing his broad back, thought with admiration that his employer was a very brave man. For Howard Appleton was walking in the shadow of death. Only that evening he had accepted the post of police commissioner of the City of New York—a post which, to Frank Dunning's mind, carried with it the threat of death. Appleton was the third incumbent of that position in the last ten days.

Young Dunning's mind flew back to the first of those two. Patrick Sargent had been found dead of poison two days after being appointed; and there was little reason to suspect that Sargent had taken his own life. Then, Harlan Foote, the second appointee, had suddenly been afflicted with a mental ailment

1

that required his removal to an insane asylum. Now, Howard Appleton, a former fighting District Attorney of New York County, had accepted the job.

Dunning's eyes were troubled. But momentarily he forgot his caution as he saw his employer safely on the top step, thumbing

Wentworth blazed
away at the driver.

the buzzer. He breathed a sigh of relief, got into the limousine, and started away.

Neither he nor Appleton saw the two slowly moving sedans

that crawled up Madison Avenue. The first warning they had was the wicked, spatting sound of a silenced revolver.

A black hole appeared as if by magic between Appleton's shoulder blades. He uttered a tortured gasp and clutched at his throat. Blood suddenly flecked his lips. He tried to shout, but no sound came from his throat except a muted gurgle. He staggered, his knees buckled under him, and he collapsed before his own door. He twitched convulsively, stiffened—and lay still.

The Honorable Howard Appleton, formerly District Attorney, and newly appointed Commissioner of Police, was dead.

SEVERAL PEOPLE passing in the street began to shout. Frank Dunning braked the limousine to a stop and leaped to the pavement. He sprang across the sidewalk and up the three short stairs to kneel beside the body of his employer. The two slowly moving cars which had just passed also pulled up short. Four men emerged from them, two from each.

A large crowd gathered almost at once, miraculously, as if from nowhere. The two men from the first of the two cars pushed confidently through the crowd, making directly for the stoop. The second pair, lost in the crowd for a moment, soon joined their companions beside the body of Appleton.

The door of the brownstone was open now, and Appleton's manservant, Brock, appeared. Brock was tall, saturnine. No expression of any sort flickered across his face as he saw the dead body of his master. He glanced up, and his eyes flitted from one to the other of the four men who had come from the two sedans. Then his gaze rested on Dunning. He said savagely: "Damn you, Dunning, I didn't think you'd do it!"

The young chauffeur flushed, stepped around the body of Appleton and stood toe to toe with the servant, glaring at him.

His big, capable fists were knotted, and he said hotly: "You say anything like that again, Brock, and I'll shove your teeth down your lying throat!"

Brock smiled thinly and shrugged. "I'll talk at the proper time."

Police were coming from both directions on Madison Avenue now, and a radio car pulled in at the curb. A few minutes later a car from the precinct station house also arrived

Young Dunning exclaimed: "Damn you, if you think—"

The two men who had descended from the first of the passing sedans moved inconspicuously up on either side of Dunning. "That's all right, buddy. You just stick around here." Their hands gripped the chauffeur's elbows tightly.

"W-who are you?" Frank demanded. His face had gone suddenly white.

The two men flipped open their coats, exhibiting shields. "We're Sorenson and Masters of the Five-Star Detective Agency. Appleton hired us to act as bodyguards when he was appointed Commissioner. We got here just a minute too late— but in plenty of time to see enough to fry you, Mr. Chauffeur!"

"You couldn't have seen anything!" Frank Dunning exclaimed with growing consternation. "I swear I didn't kill him—"

He was interrupted by one of the two men who had alighted from the second sedan. This man was dressed in impeccable evening clothes, and he carried himself with an air of great authority. He was in his middle fifties. His name was Hugh Varner, and he  was known throughout the city as the attorney for the banking syndicate which floated municipal loans. Varner's companion was Stephen Pelton, the City Comptroller.

Varner glanced sidewise at Pelton as if for confirmation of what he was going to say, then addressed the two detectives, Sorenson and Masters. "I think if you gentlemen will look in poor Mr. Appleton's limousine, you will find evidence against this young man," he said. "We were coming to visit poor Howard, to congratulate him on his appointment, and the first thing we knew that anything was happening was when Howard fell forward with that hole in his back. Pelton and I glanced toward the limousine, and we saw Dunning here, bending over as if he were doing something at the bottom of his car. I suggest you look there—"

He stopped as Sergeant Thayer, of Homicide, pushed through the crowd. Thayer was a grizzled veteran of twenty years' service in the Department, and he had little respect for wealth or position. It was due to his extreme brusqueness, and to his dislike for toadying to those in authority, that he had not advanced beyond the position of sergeant. Now he demanded gruffly: "What happened here? Who shot Appleton?"

6

The two detectives, Sorenson and Masters, retaining their grip on Frank Dunning's elbows, quickly gave the sergeant a resume of what had occurred. Then Hugh Varner repeated his story of having seen Dunning place something in the bottom of the car.

Without a word, Thayer turned brusquely around and pushed through the crowd to where Dunning had left the limousine. He opened the door, peered in under the wheel, and whistled. The floorboard was loose, and the rubber mat that covered it was buckled in several places as if it had been replaced in a hurry. Thayer pulled back the mat, unscrewed the single nut that held the floorboard and lifted it up.

There, resting on the battery, was a long-barreled high-caliber revolver, to the muzzle of which was attached a late model silencer.

Very carefully, Thayer lifted the gun out of the receptacle, his handkerchief wrapped around the barrel. He carried it through the gaping throng, up the steps of the dead man's house, and thrust it under the nose of Frank Dunning.

He growled: "Looks like you rushed yourself a little, Dunning. You might have gotten away with it if you had smoothed out the mat a little better. I guess this will cook you."

Dunning shouted feverishly, desperately: "I didn't put it there, Sergeant. I swear to God I didn't!"

Thayer said softly: "Dunning, I arrest you for the murder of Howard Appleton. I warn you that anything you say may be used against you!"

Ten minutes had elapsed since young Frank Dunning had

driven Howard Appleton up to the curb in the limousine. Life and death had marched on inexorably in those ten minutes.

And across at the other end of town, the man who was known as the Spider did not as yet know that at that moment there was being woven a weird pattern of murder and madness and fear, which would once more drag him into the vortex of sudden peril, upon which he was about to turn his back.

CHAPTER 2
THE FOURTH APPOINTEE

IN THE beautifully appointed penthouse apartment above the small nine-story building which he owned, Richard Wentworth, *alias* the Spider, was entertaining friends at a late supper. They were seated about the snowy-white tables, sipping a priceless liqueur which Wentworth himself had brought back from Tibet years before.

Directly opposite him, at the foot of the table, sat Stanley Kirkpatrick, onetime Commissioner of Police. At Wentworth's right hand sat the woman Wentworth loved—Nita Van Sloan, whose fine-textured, copper-bronze hair reflected a hundred facets of light from the brilliant fixtures high up in the ceiling.

At Wentworth's left sat a little girl, golden-haired, demure. She was no more than ten, but she bore herself with all the grace of a great lady. Purposely, she was modeling herself upon the gestures and mannerisms of her heroine, Nita Van Sloan. This little girl was Elaine Robillard. Not so long ago, a dreadful blight had descended upon the city in the shape of one who called himself the Living Pharaoh. Wentworth and Nita had fought this Living Pharaoh through three months of cruel, merciless warfare. In the end they had conquered; but one of the casualties was little Elaine Robillard, who had been left an orphan. Now, Nita Van Sloan had adopted the child. It was a gesture indicative of Nita's steadfast love of Wentworth. For, since he had dedicated his life to a constant battle against crime, there could be no marital happiness for either of them. Nita found her natural urge for motherhood partially satisfied by the adoption of Elaine.

There were three other men in the room. They were Wentworth's personal servants. One, a huge, bearded Sikh, was garbed in the traditional costume of the high-caste Hindu, with a ceremonial turban wound about his head. His long beard was carefully trimmed, and a jewel-hilted dagger rested in a sheath at his belt. The other two were Jenkyns, his butler, and Jackson, his chauffeur.

All three of these men were as devoted to Richard Wentworth as it is possible for one human being to be to another. Jenkyns had served Wentworth's father before him. Jackson had been under Major Wentworth's command in France, and the ties that lay between them were far greater than those of master and servant. As for Ram Singh, the Sikh came from a long line of warriors, and his fierce pride was a thing he would defend with his life. Yet he found it not inconsistent to be in the service of Richard Wentworth, whom he respected as a warrior greater than himself.

Jenkyns had just finished pouring the liqueur, and was resting with the decanter. Ram Singh and Jackson had entered the room a moment before, and were standing at the door.

Ex-Commissioner Kirkpatrick was about to raise his glass, when Wentworth stopped him. "Just a moment, Kirk. I have an announcement to make. But first—" He arose, pushing his chair back, and faced his three servants. His voice assumed the curt ring of command. "Jenkyns! Jackson! Ram Singh!"

THE THREE loyal servants drew themselves up to attention. Wentworth went on: "Jenkyns, you will pour three more liqueurs, and set three more chairs at the table. Then, you three will seat yourselves."

The old butler looked slightly dismayed. Jackson was shocked. And Ram Singh spread his hands, palms upward, in a gesture of negation. "Nay, *sahib*, we are but servants," he protested. "A servant does not sit at the same board with his master!"

Wentworth's eyes were glowing, and his voice throbbed with emotion. "You three are far more than servants. We have all gone through so much together that there can be no question of master and servant between us. Seat yourselves."

"But, sir," Jenkyns exclaimed, "it's against all precedent—"

"We can listen to you standing up, Major," Jackson said.

"And it will be more seemly," Ram Singh added, "in deference to your distinguished company." He bowed slightly toward Commissioner Stanley Kirkpatrick.

Richard Wentworth's eyes regarded the three affectionately. A smile hovered at his lips, but he quickly suppressed it. Sternly he rapped: "An end to this discussion. You will seat yourselves. It is an order!"

Larrabie suddenly stiffened, then heaved against Kirkpatrick.

Ram Singh glanced at the other two servants, then shrugged his shoulders helplessly. "If it is an order, *sahib*, that is different. An order is an order."

Reluctantly, Jenkyns set three more places, and poured some of the golden brown liqueur into three additional glasses Then, as if celebrating a special rite, the three took their places at the table—Sam Singh and Jackson on the side at which Nita sat, and Jenkyns next to little golden-haired Elaine Robillard. They sat stiffly, ill at ease.

Elaine clapped her hands gleefully. "Fine! Now we are all like a great big family. Jenkyns is nice, and so is Jackson. But I like Ram Singh best. He lets me pull his beard!"

They all smiled, and then Richard Wentworth got to his feet. He looked around the table slowly.

Elaine Robillard knew him only as Richard Wentworth, a wealthy gentleman who had been incredibly good to her. Nita Van Sloan, Jackson, Jenkyns and Ram Singh knew that he was also the Spider. They had fought with him, risked their lives, with and for him, a hundred times. They were completely in his confidence, and they knew that on the occasions when Richard Wentworth disappeared unaccountably from his usual haunts, somewhere the Spider was working alone against crime.

Stanley Kirkpatrick was the only one who did not know definitely that he was the Spider. As Commissioner of Police, Kirkpatrick had waged a relentless war against that scourge of the underworld. He more than suspected his true identity, and when he was Commissioner he had as much as told Wentworth that if he ever got the goods on the Spider he would prosecute him without mercy; for the Spider's unorthodox method of dealing with criminals had placed him outside the pale of the law. But on many an occasion the two blazing guns of that mysterious and dreaded character had cut short the cruel and vicious lives of underworld nabobs whom the red tape of the law had been unable to reach.

Now Richard Wentworth saw that the faces of all these people were fixed upon him questioningly. They were wondering what important announcement he was about to make, and for which he had set the stage so carefully. He spoke to them in a low voice which barely carried beyond the bounds of the table.

"My friends," he said, "we have all of us lived through some very perilous and some very exciting times. In our association we have learned to love and respect one another. You, Kirk, were a brave and efficient police commissioner. No one can blame you if you resigned at last, because you are richly entitled to the rest that you are going to enjoy. In the war with the man who called himself the Living Pharaoh, we were all close to death. By a miracle we triumphed, and now the city is rid of the menace of that super-criminal.

"I, too, want a rest. I feel that the time has come when I can retire from the work that I have been doing. The underworld is quiet, except for a few occasional crimes. Ram Singh, Jackson, Jenkyns, I am releasing you three from service. I have established a trust fund for all of you, which will give you an income amply sufficient to live in comfort for the rest of your lives."

There was a stunned silence around the table. It was broken at last by Jackson.

"But, sir, you can't let us go," he burst out. "It's not the money we want. You know we'd never be happy if we weren't working for you—"

Wentworth raised a hand to silence him. He glanced down at Nita Van Sloan, and she nodded, lowering her eyes. Wentworth smiled and addressed the gathering once more. "The reason I am releasing you three from service will become apparent when I make the next announcement. Nita and I are going to be married. We are going to take Elaine with us on a cruise around the world!"

Slowly, Wentworth sat down and placed a hand over Nita's slim one. Little Elaine cried out joyously: "Hurrah! Hurrah! We'll see all those beautiful countries that they tell about in the geography book!"

JENKYNS FURTIVELY brushed the back of his hand across his eyes. Jackson was grinning broadly. And Ram Singh said in his deep booming voice: *"Inshallah!* It is a good thing. There are no two in the world who would make a better match. We three servants will resign ourselves to live alone."

Stanley Kirkpatrick arose from his seat. His voice was a bit unsteady. "You two have richly deserved this. I trust that you will lead a full and happy life." He raised his liqueur glass, and his eyes rested on Nita. "I drink to a most brave and beautiful lady!"

They all raised their glasses and drank the toast. Then Wentworth leaned over and kissed Nita lightly on the lips.

Ram Singh said with a sly look in his eyes: "And the Spider, Master? What of the Spider? Does he, too, retire?"

They all tensed, watching Wentworth. His face suddenly became hard. He said harshly: "The Spider, my friends, is dead! Let him remain the myth and the legend that he always has been. Let us forget that there ever was such a person as the Spider."

Kirkpatrick sighed. "Let's drink one more toast," he said. "Let's drink to the hope that the Spider will never walk again!"

Just then, the buzzer in the foyer rang, announcing a caller. They looked at each other questioningly. Nita Van Sloan grew pale. She put an impulsive hand on Wentworth's sleeve.

"Dick! Don't answer it! I have a strange feeling. Something tells me it's—"

Abruptly, her voice dropped. "Dick, I knew it was too good to be true." The words came from her lips as if she were uttering a dire prophecy. "I'm afraid—the Spider—*will*—walk again!"

THE BUZZER sounded once more, and Jenkyns half rose from his seat, glancing at Wentworth for instructions. Dick nodded, and the old servant made his way around the table, left the room in the direction of the foyer. The others sat silent. They were all impressed by the sudden feeling of foreboding which had assailed Nita. They knew very well from past experience that those premonitions of hers usually bore fruit.

In a moment, Jenkyns returned and announced: "Mayor Larrabie calling to see Mr. Wentworth—"

He was interrupted by the abrupt entrance of a short, stocky, florid-faced man. This was Mayor Phillips Larrabie, who had been elected only recently on a reform ticket following the sweeping revulsion of the city at the long list of crimes which the previous administration had countenanced. Larrabie had sworn, upon taking office, to rid the city of crime and to drive every member of the underworld out of the Metropolitan District. But so far he had been unable to find a commissioner to take the job of directing the Police Department in its work.

Now Larrabie advanced quickly into the room, walking with short, jerky steps. He glanced around the room, nodded in satisfaction when he saw Kirkpatrick, then hurried over to Wentworth and grasped his hand. He spoke in the quick, sharp accent of a busy man who always knew what he wanted and went after it as directly as he could.

"You must excuse me for breaking in on you this way, Wentworth. I assure you that only a grave emergency would have induced me to do so."

Wentworth smiled tolerantly, and pressed the Mayor's hand. "You're always welcome here, Larrabie. I want you to meet Miss Van Sloan, my fiancée, little Elaine Robillard, Ram Singh, Jackson, and Jenkyns. You know Stanley Kirkpatrick, of course. These are all old friends of mine, and I'm sure they will all join me in asking you to have a drink with us, especially as Miss Van Sloan and I are soon to be married, and make a trip around the world."

"No, no," Larrabie said quickly. "Nothing would please me more than to drink with you, but you must excuse me. I've come here on an extremely serious matter." His gaze met squarely that of the ex-commissioner across the length of the table. "Stanley Kirkpatrick, I would like to talk to you privately. No doubt, these good people will excuse us—"

Kirkpatrick stretched a hand across toward him. "Sit down, Larrabie. I have no secrets from anyone in this room. You must feel free to talk before them."

Larrabie bit his lip in vexation, then shrugged and took the seat which Jenkyns had provided for him.

"All right!" he snapped. "I called your home, and they told me you were here so I came directly, without telephoning. I'll tell you what I want in a nutshell." He leaned over the table, and there was a queer gleam in his eye. "Stanley Kirkpatrick, I want to appoint you Police Commissioner of New York City. And I want you to accept!"

Kirkpatrick's face set sternly. "No, Larrabie. I won't do it. I've been through enough, and I'm going to take a rest. There are plenty of men in New York who will be glad to take the job. You don't need me."

"But I *do* need you, Kirkpatrick. I need you badly. I'm going to give you an idea of how badly I need you." Larrabie kicked back his chair and arose. He placed both hands on the table and leaned over to emphasize his words. "Six days ago I appointed Patrick Sargent police commissioner. He died of poison. Four

17

days ago I appointed Harlan Foote to the post of Commissioner. Foote became insane."

Kirkpatrick nodded. "We all know that. They were unfortunate occurrences—"

Larrabie smiled twistedly. "You think they were accidents? Let me tell you this. Today I appointed Howard Appleton to the commissionership. *At eleven forty-two o'clock tonight, Howard Appleton was shot to death on the steps of his own home!*"

Larrabie waited while the full force of that announcement struck home to those around the table. Silently, Richard Wentworth and Nita Van Sloan exchanged understanding glances. This was the thing that Nita had feared when the doorbell sounded. When catastrophe struck three times like this in quick succession, it could be no accident. There was something deeply sinister underlying the sudden madness of one, and the death of two newly appointed police commissioners.

LARRABIE NODDED, reading their thoughts. "You get the idea. There is something more than appears on the surface here. There've been a few isolated holdups in the city during the last week, crimes that might be attributed to occasional gangsters. But I think that they are directed from a single source— the same source that is eliminating each new commissioner as fast as I appoint him.

"There've been rumors in the underworld about a hooded master—a dictator of the underworld, a man who intends to force me or trick me into eventually appointing a police commissioner whom he can handle. I'm going to fool this dictator. I'm going to appoint Stanley Kirkpatrick as commissioner."

Nita Van Sloan exclaimed: "You want to put Kirk in danger? If three men have already been killed, what is there to prevent Mr. Kirkpatrick from meeting the same fate?"

Larrabie sighed. "Yes, I'm putting Kirk on the spot. But I think I'm outsmarting this dictator by doing it this way. Do you know why?"

Kirkpatrick looked uneasily across the table at Wentworth and Nita, but said nothing.

Larrabie went on impetuously: "You see, I know that while Kirkpatrick was in charge of the Police Department, a certain very notorious character was very active in aiding him against the underworld."

He spoke slowly now, as if wishing to impress every word he said upon his hearers. And as he spoke, he allowed his gaze to travel around the table and to rest significantly upon Wentworth.

"That notorious character was the Spider. I feel that if Kirkpatrick becomes commissioner, the Spider will take an interest in the situation. And, my friends, I think the situation is serious enough to warrant such intervention. As an officer of the law, as the chief executive of this city, I cannot openly enlist the services of the Spider. But I *can* appoint the Spider's best friend as Commissioner!"

Kirkpatrick wiped perspiration from his forehead. "What makes you think that the Spider is my friend? Do you—er—know who the Spider is?"

Larrabie smiled twistedly. "I have a good idea—" once more his gaze returned to Wentworth—"but I wouldn't want to make a statement unsupported by fact. I will say, however, that if the Spider is looking for excitement, he will find it in this city, *without taking any trip around the world.*"

Wentworth stiffened. Larrabie, like some few others, guessed that he was the Spider. Wentworth was not worried by that so much as by the sudden challenge that had been laid at his door by Larrabie.

And in the eyes of Nita Van Sloan there was a sudden dawning fear. When Richard Wentworth looked like that, he wasn't thinking of love, or of trips around the world, or of peaceful and complacent happiness; he was thinking of battle, of swift adventure and of sudden death. And Nita's heart throbbed in fierce revolt beneath her breast. Now, on the threshold of happiness, she was to be denied it. Why, *why* did this thing have to come up just at this moment? Couldn't Larrabie have waited until tomorrow? By that time they would have been on the high seas. **KIRKPATRICK WAS** talking now, low-voiced, moody. "So you want me on the job, Larrabie, in order to enlist the support of the Spider? You hope that the Spider will exert himself to protect me, and in event that I'm killed, you think that the Spider will avenge me by going after this dictator of yours?"

Larrabie struck the table with his fist. "By God, Kirkpatrick, I'll protect you plenty. I'm not going to have the same thing happen to you that happened to the other three. If you accept, you're coming downtown with me, and I'll give you a bodyguard of the best men the Department has. Not only that, but I'll give you a free hand. Regardless of whether the Spider comes into this or not, you are the only man who can cope with the present situation.

"Kirkpatrick, it's your duty to accept the job. The city needs you. *What do you say?*"

Stanley Kirkpatrick hesitated. It was very evident that a struggle was going on within him. He had been through a good deal in the days of the hectic fight against the Living Pharaoh. Unjustly accused of murder, he had been deprived of his position and incarcerated in jail. Only by Wentworth's clever strategy was he finally cleared of that charge. Disillusioned and weary, be had been glad to find rest in retirement. Now he was being virtually forced back into public life.

He drummed nervously with his fingertips on the table. Larrabie saw his hesitation and urged: "I've given you all the facts, Kirkpatrick. You know what you are going to face. They will try to get you, the way they got Sargent and Foote and Appleton. If I thought you were a coward, I would never have asked you in the first place, and I wouldn't have put the cards on the table the way I did."

Suddenly Kirkpatrick raised his eyes. He spoke in a low, decisive voice. "I'll take the job, Larrabie!"

The Mayor sighed in relief. "Good! I knew you wouldn't fail me. Come on. We'll go down to headquarters right now, and I will install you. And I'll see that you're damn well guarded!"

Slowly Kirkpatrick arose and walked around the table. Nita and Richard Wentworth also arose, and he shook hands with Nita, then with Wentworth. Kirkpatrick said significantly: "I don't want this to stop you, Dick, from taking that cruise around the world. I don't think it's as serious as Larrabie makes out."

Wentworth said nothing. But Nita and Kirkpatrick both knew that Wentworth would not leave for any world cruise while his friend was entering upon a period of danger.

Larrabie and Kirkpatrick drank one toast with the others to the success of the new Commissioner, and then the two of them left. When the door closed Nita said, with a catch in her voice: "Dick, does it mean—"

He looked at her somberly. "I'm afraid so, darling. Would you want me to leave now?"

She sighed. "I suppose not. I suppose I couldn't love you the way I do if you were the kind of man to leave your friend when he needs you. But it all seems so unfair!"

Dick Wentworth said nothing. He looked preoccupied. He pressed Nita's arm, said abstractedly: "This set-up doesn't look right to me. Excuse me, Nita."

He left her side swiftly, and hurried toward a corner of the room where a queer-looking mirror stood on a low table. This mirror was part of a complicated periscope arrangement by which Wentworth could see everything that went on down in the street below, as well as around both corners of the building. The periscope mirrors were arranged in a false drain pipe in such a way that it was almost impossible for the tenants of the building to notice them. From the penthouse windows there was a clear view of the Hudson River and of the Jersey shore on the other side.

But Wentworth paid no attention to that now. He gazed into

the periscope, and his face tautened. He said reflectively: "That's funny. I've never seen a hearse with portholes before."

Suddenly he jerked away from the periscope, his eyes blazing with excitement.

"Ram Singh! Jackson!" he exclaimed. "Your high-powered rifles, quick! There's a hearse slowly moving toward the doorway of this building from the corner. Stop it if you can!"

HIMSELF HE raced across the room, while Nita and Elaine Robillard watched him, wide-eyed. In the foyer he slipped open a drawer of the telephone table and snatched out two blued-steel Colt automatics, then launched himself out through the front door into the hall. Fortunately, there were two self-service elevators serving the penthouse. Wentworth had been careful to see that he had the additional elevator in case of emergency. The indicator of one of the two elevators showed that it was just passing the second floor on its way to the lobby. The second elevator was at the penthouse floor, and Wentworth swung into it, jabbed hard at the ground-floor button.

As the door swung shut, he caught a last glimpse of Ram Singh and Jackson, through the open door of the apartment. They were racing toward the terrace of the penthouse, carrying their long rifles, with which they were crack shots. Then the cage began to slide downward.

Wentworth's body was taut as he reached the ground floor. He had slipped off the safety catches on both automatics, and now he swung open the door, leaped out into the lobby, both guns thrust out straight ahead of him. At the doorway he saw Kirkpatrick and Larrabie in the act of stepping out onto the sidewalk. And just at that instant the dark bulk of the undertaker's hearse which he had glimpsed from up above came pulling slowly in front of the entrance.

Wentworth opened his mouth to shout a warning, but his cry was drowned by the sudden sharp staccato barking of machine guns.

The elevators were at a slight angle from the doorway, and Wentworth himself escaped that blast of lead. Ahead of him, he saw Larrabie suddenly stiffen, then quickly heave against Kirkpatrick, and send the Commissioner sprawling on the floor to one side of the doorway. Larrabie himself was left in the entrance, and his body caught the full blast of that machine-gun barrage.

Like a tortured thing the body of the Mayor seemed to dance in live agony as wave after wave of hot lead slammed into him. Wentworth uttered a hoarse cry and raised his automatics, sent twin streaks of blue flame searing in the direction of the hearse. His slugs rebounded harmlessly from shatterproof glass. He saw four open portholes from which four machine guns dealt lead. He also saw a man in the driver's seat crouching over the wheel, and beside him another man whose face and head were covered by a black hood.

Wentworth swerved his guns from the useless fusillade against the bulletproof glass, and aimed for the driver. He had only one shot left in each automatic, and he fired each in quick succession. The driver's head seemed to disintegrate under the two powerfully-propelled slugs. The hearse swerved, careened, and the machine-gun fire suddenly ceased.

Larrabie was on the tiled floor now, writhing feebly, a spark of life still in his eyes.

Kirkpatrick was picking himself up from the floor where Larrabie had thrust him. The Commissioner was crawling toward the entrance on all fours. Being in evening dress, he had come unarmed, and had no gun.

Wentworth's guns were useless, for he had fired the last shot. But he leaped over the body of the still-quivering Larrabie, and raced out into the open in time to see the truck, out of control, swerve and smash head-on into the lamppost thirty feet beyond the doorway.

From the driver's seat the figure of a man suddenly erupted. It was the man who wore the hood. He leaped to the ground and ran, zigzag, diagonally across the street into the safety of the shadows of Riverside Park, on the opposite side. In a moment he had disappeared down the steep slope of the cliff.

The four men who had operated the machine guns within the hearse leaped out of it and dashed after the hooded man. They had left their machine guns in order the better to escape. But now they were pulling revolvers out of their shoulder holsters.

Wentworth disregarded the danger of those revolvers, and raced after the four fleeing men. One of them turned, snarling, and leveled a gun at him. But the man never had an opportunity to fire. For at that moment a rain of lead spattered onto the sidewalk on all sides of him as well as around the other three gunmen. Ram Singh and Jackson were firing swiftly, with deadly precision, from the penthouse overhead.

The two thugs nearest to Wentworth fell, riddled with bullets.

The other two ran a few more paces, reached the edge of the cliff above the railroad tracks, and then toppled over into space as more slugs from the rifles of the two men on the roof pounded into them.

Wentworth smiled tightly, but there was a bit of disappointment in that smile. Ram Singh and Jackson had surely saved his life, but the hooded man who must have been the leader of the gang had escaped. He shrugged, left the bodies of the dead gunmen in the middle of the street, and hurried around to the front of the hearse.

THE RADIATOR was entirely smashed in, and clouds of hot steam were pouring from it. The dead man behind the wheel was unrecognizable, for both of Wentworth's bullets had gone through his head, tearing away most of his face. Richard Wentworth reached in grimly and turned off the ignition, in order to prevent the hearse from catching fire. Then he turned and strode back into the building. His eyes were bleak and hard as he knelt beside the dying Mayor Larrabie. On the other side of him knelt Kirkpatrick. The Commissioner's hands were trembling, and there was sweat on his forehead.

"My God!" Kirkpatrick exclaimed. "He gave up his life to save me. If he hadn't pushed me out of the way, I'd have got it too!"

Wentworth nodded. "Yes, I saw it. It was a brave thing to do. Larrabie—was a man!"

Abruptly he knelt lower, as he saw the Mayor's eyes flickering, and his lips moving feebly. A mumble was coming from Larrabie's mouth now, mingled with the gurgling of blood in his larynx. The tiled floor was being stained a deep crimson by his life's blood. But there was an uncanny perseverance, a stubborn courage that kept the man alive until he had spoken what he wanted to say. Now his lips were forming a message that he was trying desperately to get across. Wentworth caught these words:

"I—saved Kirk's life—because—he's needed—more than I, and I—promised him protection…" A wry smile pinched at Larrabie's pallid lips. "I—made—good. Now he must fight for me—must fight the Dictator… I wish—to God—the Spider—would help him too…."

A police whistle was sounding outside, and Wentworth motioned to Kirkpatrick, who arose and went to the doorway to meet the uniformed men who had come running. The elevator indicator showed that one of the cages was at the fifth floor on its way down. For a moment or two Wentworth would be alone with the dying Mayor. He bent low, and said clearly, strongly. "Larrabie! Can you hear me?"

The spunky Mayor's eyelids flickered. *"If the Spider would only help!"*

Wentworth suddenly said through clenched teeth: "Larrabie, the Spider will help. You have my word for it. The Spider will avenge you!"

A sudden access of energy seemed to surge through the Mayor's body. "You—promise it? How do I know—"

The exertion was too much for him. He dropped back to the floor from which he had pulled himself up, and lay panting.

Wentworth said softly: "This is how you can know it, Larrabie." From his pocket he extracted a platinum cigarette lighter. Swiftly he unscrewed the back of it, exposing a small seal. He pressed this seal upon a drop of the blood that spattered the floor, and said: *"Look!"*

There, perfectly etched in the smear of blood, was a miniature replica of a spider—the seal of the man who was known and feared throughout the underworld.

Larrabie's eyes widened. He had seen that seal upon the foreheads of many dead men during the past years. He knew that whenever the Spider "executed" a dangerous underworld character he left that seal of his handiwork upon the man's forehead. And he knew now that Richard Wentworth was the Spider.

A slow, happy smile spread upon his pain-wracked features. For a moment it seemed as if he suffered no agony whatsoever. His eyes brightened, and he spoke clearly. "Now I can die. Now I know I have not died in vain. Remember, Spider, you—have promised—to avenge me."

Larrabie's eyes closed as if he were weary, and a tremendous spasm racked his body. A gurgle sounded in his throat, and he stiffened, his eyes opening wide, staring upward emptily. He was dead.

CHAPTER 3
THE SPIDER WALKS AGAIN

POLICE WERE pushing in from the street past Kirkpatrick; Ram Singh and Jackson were coming out of the door of the self-service elevator. Wentworth arose swiftly, and scraped his foot over the spot of blood where he had imprinted the seal of the Spider.

His eye alighted on the corner of a paper of some sort that was protruding from the inner pocket of Larrabie's dress suit. He bent and drew it out.

A hand grasped his shoulder.

A plainclothes detective, who had just come in, seized him by the arm and whirled him around. "Say, you, what do you think you're doing?"

The sight of the dead body of the Mayor had caused the police to see red; and now they were gruffly herding everyone into a corner of the lobby. The plainclothes detective raised a clenched fist to strike Wentworth. "You give me that paper—"

Kirkpatrick interrupted. "It's all right, Dennison," he said mildly. "Mr. Wentworth is—"

Dennison swung on him, snarling. "Never you mind, Mr. Kirkpatrick. We ain't taking orders from you. You're not the commissioner anymore. This is a case of murder, and I'm going to act—"

He was interrupted by the soft voice of Richard Wentworth, who had unfolded the document taken from Larrabie's coat. "You will excuse me, Detective Dennison, but you are mistaken in your facts. You *are* taking orders from Commissioner Kirkpatrick whether you like it or not. Here is a certified document, signed and attested at the City Hall, which Mayor Larrabie must have executed before coming here. It is an order appointing Stanley Kirkpatrick Commissioner of Police. That means, my friend, that you will take orders from Commissioner Kirkpatrick until Mayor Larrabie's successor appoints another commissioner!"

Dennison turned back to Wentworth, his mouth agape. Dick held up the paper so that the detective could read it.

Kirkpatrick said in an awed voice: "Larrabie knew I'd never be able to refuse him. He had the appointment all drawn up!"

Dennison saluted awkwardly. "Sorry, Commissioner. I hope you will overlook what I said before. I never knew—"

"That's all right, Dennison. Now suppose you get around and organize this thing, and leave Mr. Wentworth alone."

Kirkpatrick, now that he was commissioner, swung with smooth ease and efficiency into the discharge of his duties. He gave crisp orders, and in a moment it seemed that he had never been out of the Police Department.

While he was directing the handling of the body and the setting up of police lines outside to keep the crowds of curious away, Wentworth drew Ram Singh and Jackson out of the building to the sidewalk. He frowned at them. "What happened to you two?" he asked. "You had the rifles—"

Ram Singh lowered his eyes. "Master, only one escaped us— the one with the hood. Of the others, two lie dead here in the street, and the other two have fallen over the side of the cliff. But the man in the hood escaped, because we shot at those others first. We wished to protect you."

Before Wentworth could speak, Nita Van Sloan came hurrying out of the building. She had thrown a cloak over her shoulders, and Wentworth's heart skipped a beat as the full force of her beauty struck him, flushed as she was with excitement and the scent of danger. Her eyes were wide, and she came up to Wentworth, put both hands on his chest. "Dick! You're all right?"

He nodded grimly. "I'm all right, darling. But Larrabie got it. It was only by a miracle that Kirk is still alive. Larrabie sacrificed his own life to save Kirk."

Nita said: "What now, Dick? Our plans—they're all wrecked?"

Soberly, he inclined his head. "I'm afraid so, darling. This looks like war. It seems that everything Larrabie said is true. And I've sworn to avenge him."

Nita faced him bravely. "All right, then. We'll work together—"

She stopped, and her face grew pale. He was shaking his head, smiling grimly.

"No, Nita, we won't work together. I—I've been a fool, letting you risk your life all those other times. Darling, you're too precious to me. If anything happened to you, I—I don't think I could go on. And I've no right to let Ram Singh and Jackson take such terrible risks. From now on—" his voice became hard, with a decisive finality—"from now on, the Spider walks alone."

Nita bowed her head. She recognized that tone. There would be no use arguing the matter with Wentworth now. But Ram Singh and Jackson both broke into voluble protestations at once.

Wentworth frowned, and ejaculated sharply: "Ram Singh! Jackson! I have made up my mind. There is no use arguing. I will not expose my friends to any further risks. I'm leaving now. You won't hear from me until this is over."

He grasped Ram Singh's hand, pressed it warmly, then shook Jackson's hand. "I will expect you both to take good care of Nita. I want nothing to happen to her."

He turned from them, and drew Nita Van Sloan into his arms. Bravely, she smiled up at him as he held her warm, throbbing body close against him. For a moment the whole world dissolved away from these two as they stood there. Wentworth's lips meet Nita's in a long kiss, and she clung to him, her small hands gripping hard at his shoulders as if to keep him from leaving her. At last he tore his lips away from hers.

"Dick! Dick, dear! Must you do it this way? Can't you let me fight by your side—"

"No, darling. I want to know that you'll be safe and alive when I come back. Goodbye, darling. Tell Kirkpatrick to go ahead full blast with every facility of the Department against this Dictator. Tell him that the Spider will be working too!"

And Wentworth twisted out of Nita's arms, raised a hand to Ram Singh and Jackson, and hurried quickly up the street.

The three of them gazed after his broad back for a long moment And then Nita Van Sloan suddenly came out of the daze in which his abrupt departure had left her. Her voice throbbed with urgency. "Ram Singh! Jackson! Go after him.

RICHARD WENTWORTH

Follow him everywhere. I am afraid for him. I know—he goes into great danger."

Ram Singh's eyes gleamed with eagerness, and Jackson smiled broadly. "You want us to stay on his trail all the time?"

"Yes, yes. I shall be in no danger. But I have a feeling—that this Dictator is stronger than Dick imagines. Stay with him, you two. Never leave him out of your sight. But don't let him know you're following him."

Ram Singh and Jackson needed no second urging. Jackson saluted stiffly, Ram Singh salaamed, and then they both slipped away into the night after the fast-disappearing figure of Richard Wentworth.

For a long time after they had gone Nita Van Sloan stood there in the street, regardless of the bustling police and the newspaper reporters, of the crowds of curious who had gathered around the building. Her little hands were clenched hard at her side, and she blinked her eyes to keep back the suspicion of tears that welled within them. Then, abruptly, raising her chin, she turned back and reentered the building....

IN A room in the basement of police headquarters on Center Street in New York City, curly-headed young Frank Dunning sat in a chair under a powerful light that nearly blinded him. The room was bare of furniture except for a single table and chair at which sat a police stenographer. Grouped about Dunning's chair were three plainclothes detectives, together with Sergeant Thayer and Inspector Strong, the head of the Homicide Squad.

"You've got to talk!" Thayer was saying. "By God, you'll stay here all night and all day tomorrow if you don't talk. I tell you, Dunning, you'll wish you'd never been born if you don't come across with the dope!"

Dunning raised haggard eyes to the sergeant. His hair was ruffled, and there was a bloody crack across his lips. He had the look of a desperate, cornered animal.

"I swear to God, Sergeant, I didn't kill Mr. Appleton. I tell you, I don't know a thing about that gun. I don't know how it got in the car—"

Thayer's rasping laughter cut across Dunning's frantic protestations of innocence. "You can't get away with that stuff, Dunning. Brock, the butler, says you asked Appleton for a raise last week, and you were sore as hell when you didn't get it. He says you told him you'd like to knock Appleton's block off. Did you say that, or didn't you?"

"It wasn't anything like that," the young chauffeur wailed. "I just said it was a shame he wouldn't give a fellow a raise. I'd been with him six months, and he was only paying me twenty-two dollars—"

"You didn't feel like that when you got the job," Thayer interrupted. "Your uncle, Argyle Dunning, the President of the Board of Aldermen, got you that job with Appleton, didn't he?"

"That's true. My uncle got me the job and I was grateful. I never said I'd knock Mr. Appleton's block off. Brock is lying." He looked up beseechingly. "Won't one of you please get in touch with my uncle? He'll help me—"

"Nix. Argyle Dunning isn't going to know anything about where you're being held, until you're arraigned in court tomorrow. We're not letting him send any high-priced lawyers in here to drag you out."

Inspector Strong, who had been watching from a few feet away, now stepped forward. He spoke in the soothing voice of a father-confessor.

"Why don't you confess, my boy? I'm sure it will go easier with you if you do. You won't have a leg to stand on when you go on trial for murder, if you don't come clean with us. Those two detectives, Sorenson and Masters, claim they saw you fire the gun. The bullet in Appleton's body was checked by the Ballistics Bureau, and there's no doubt at all that it was fired from that gun you had in the car. Not only that, but Hugh Varner and Comptroller Pelton both testify they saw you hiding the gun in the battery compartment. It's an airtight case, Dunning. You'd do well to come clean."

Frank's voice rose in a hysterical shriek. "I won't confess! I tell you, I won't confess. I won't admit doing something I never had a hand in. Sorenson and Masters are lying. Varner and Pelton were mistaken. I never shot Appleton, and I never put that gun in the car."

Strong exchanged significant glances with Sergeant Thayer. Then the Inspector said flatly: "All right, Thayer. If that's the way he feels about it, go to work on him!"

Sergeant Thayer grinned smugly. "Okay, Inspector. We'll give him the works—from soup to nuts. Before we are through with him, he'll be begging to talk!"

"I needn't tell you," Strong cautioned, "to be careful. Don't leave any marks that will show in court tomorrow."

Thayer nodded. "The boys know their business, Inspector. Leave everything to us."

Dunning plunged up from his seat. "Damn you, leave me alone! I'm innocent—"

Thayer's fist crashed full into his face, sending him smashing back into the seat, sobbing in frantic helplessness. Thayer nodded to the three plainclothesmen. "Go to work, boys."

Inspector Strong started for the door, but stopped when he heard a discreet tap, and a uniformed attendant entered with

a slip of paper. The
man's holster at his
side was empty of its
revolver, and his face
bore a flushed, excited,
half-terrified expres-
sion.

Inspector Strong
rapped out, frowning: "What's the matter, Griggs?"

The man exclaimed: "Gawd, Inspector! The Spider was just
here!"

"The Spider! He was here—and he got away?"

"Y-yes, sir. He suddenly appeared out of nowhere in the
Charge Room, and he pulled a gun on us and made us all line
up against the wall. Then he stuck a piece of paper in the type-
writer and typed a message. It's for you. He backed out of the
room and got away before we could do a thing. He took all our
guns with him."

Inspector Strong grated: "You're a fine bunch of guys. Letting
one man get away with a thing like that! So the Spider is back,
is he? Let's see that note!"

He snatched the slip of paper from Griggs. At the top
appeared the imprint of the Spider's seal. Below it were written
the following terse lines:

> You are wasting your time with Dunning. Masters and Soren-
> son are lying. Varner and Pelton are either lying or mistaken.
> Dunning is innocent. I know that you are putting him through

the third degree without the knowledge of Commissioner Kirk-patrick. You are doing this either through stupidity or malice. If it is stupidity, take warning and cease now. If it is through malice, you will have to answer to the Spider. Here is a tip for you: concentrate on Sorenson and Masters rather than on Dunning!

There was no signature on the note, but it needed none. The imprint of the Spider's seal at the top was sufficient to identify it.

Strong swore softly under his breath and read the grim message aloud to Sergeant Thayer. The two of them glanced around to make sure they were not overheard, then moved over to a corner and whispered between themselves.

Finally Thayer shrugged and said: "Kirkpatrick phoned that he wouldn't be back at headquarters for another hour. We have an hour to work on this kid. To hell with the Spider! If we can break Dunning down and make him confess, it will practically close the case."

Inspector Strong nodded. "Go ahead. If Kirkpatrick comes and finds out about it, you can refer him to me. I'll take the blame. I know how to handle that baby!"

Thayer nodded and turned back toward Dunning, grinning evilly. Inspector Strong went out and issued swift orders to the Broadcast Room to notify all radio cars to be on the lookout for the Spider.

"He's gone too far, invading police headquarters like this. Give out a statement," he ordered Griggs, "for publication in the newspapers. Say that the Spider raided headquarters and wounded one of our men. We'll get the public turned against that guy. There won't be anybody in the city will have any sympathy for him when we catch him and shoot him down!"

Inspector Strong hurried into his office, closed and locked the door, then picked up his own private telephone, which was not connected through the headquarters switchboard. He dialed a number; then, when his connection was made, he said cautiously: "Hello, this is Number Twenty-seven talking. I have a report to make…."

IN A richly furnished room in a tall building overlooking the Public Library of New York City, a telephone bell tinkled musically. The walls of this room were covered with rich hangings which screened even the doorway. The furniture was expensive and richly upholstered, and the rug was thick and luxurious.

At one wall, directly opposite the window which looked out across the library, was a broad desk of carved mahogany, into which had been worked the figures of tawny-maned lions. On the hanging behind the desk, which was a drape of purest cloth of gold, was emblazoned a heraldic design. It consisted of the figure of a lion seated upon a golden crown. The lion's forepaws were outstretched, and in one paw it held a sword while in the other it held a miter.

The chair behind the desk was suggestive of a throne. It was massive, with a high back upon which the emblem of the lion was repeated.

A man sat in this chair. He was impeccably garbed, dressed in evening clothes, but his hands were gloved, and his head was covered by a hood. The soft, indirect lighting of the room left the eyes behind the slit in the hood in deep shadow.

Opposite him sat a woman, beautiful in a dark, exotic way. Black hair was coiled in a deep mass at the back of her head and over her ears, from which hung long emerald earrings. The white skin of her throat and bosom was daringly revealed by an extremely low-cut, brilliant red gown. Long, dark-lashed eyes gazed steadily at the hooded man. Small red lips formed a flash of crimson in an otherwise white face.

She did not move as the telephone rang, but the man behind the desk broke off in the act of speaking to her, made a gesture of impatience, and picked up the phone. His voice was harsh, abrupt, as he spoke into the instrument: "Yes?"

Over the wire came the voice of Inspector Strong: "This is Number Twenty-seven talking. I have a report to make."

"You may speak, Twenty-seven," said the hooded man.

Inspector Strong's voice came over the phone once more. It no longer had the ring of authority with which the Inspector spoke when at headquarters. "We have Dunning downstairs, but we haven't been able to make him talk yet. The Spider just visited headquarters—"

"What?" The hooded man's gloved hand tightened on the instrument. "Repeat that!"

"I said, sir, the Spider just visited us at headquarters. He left me a note."

"Read it to me!"

Quickly, Strong obeyed.

The hooded man spoke harshly into the phone: "You are a fool, Number Twenty-seven. You have allowed yourself to be hoodwinked. Did I not instruct you that you were to have Dunning's signed confession in court tomorrow *at all costs?*"

"But, sir, I did my best. I threatened, and I cajoled. He's stubborn. But Thayer and the boys will break him down—"

"You fool! They won't break him down anymore. Did you read that note from the Spider aloud in Dunning's presence?"

"I did."

"Don't you see, you idiot, that the Spider wanted you to do just that? He knew you were down there with Dunning. He did it that way to make it spectacular, so you would be taken by surprise and read the note right there. It contains nothing that he couldn't have told you by calling you on the telephone. His purpose was to give Dunning enough courage to resist, to withstand the third degree. And he succeeded. Now Dunning knows the Spider is behind him. Dunning also knows that as soon as Kirkpatrick learns he is being held there, he will be released from the third degree. That is all the Spider wanted to accomplish!"

Inspector Strong's voice came over the phone now, much weaker, much less sure of himself. "I—I'm sorry, sir. I didn't think of that. It took me by surprise—"

"Of course it did. I am displeased with you, Number Twenty-seven. Do you know what it means when I am displeased with one of my numbers?"

"No, no, sir! I beg you, be merciful. I'll do better next time. I'll do anything you say. Give me another chance—"

"I seldom give another chance. In this case I will be lenient. Let Thayer and the others do what they can. And in the meantime use every means at your disposal to capture the Spider. Hold yourself in readiness for further orders."

The hooded man carefully replaced the phone in its cradle. For a long time there was utter silence in the dimly lit room, while he seemed to be meditating. The dark-haired, white-skinned woman opposite him said nothing, but watched through veiled eyes. There was a slight hint of a smile upon her carmine lips as minutes ticked into minutes while the hooded man was lost in meditation.

AT LAST he spoke. "My dear Olga, I have made a serious mistake."

She raised her eyebrows in mock surprise. "What! Is it possible that the clever, unscrupulous, infallible Count Calypsa has actually made a mistake—"

She stopped, choking back the rest of her words. The hooded man was leaning forward in his seat, with hands clenched in anger.

"Stop!" he thundered. "I have forbidden you ever to mention that name." His voice dropped suddenly, became sulky, threatening. "I think, my dear Olga, that you presume too much upon our past acquaintance. One of these days you will go too far—and there will be no turning back for you."

Olga smiled tauntingly at him across the desk. "I know, dear Count. One of these days I will die, just as so many others who have displeased you have already died. But for the present I think I am safe—because you still need me. When my usefulness to the Dictator is over, I shall prepare for death."

The hooded man's hands slowly unclenched on the desk. He

lost his tenseness. "Let us hope for your sake, dearest Olga, that you will remain useful to me for a long time."

"Believe me," she said earnestly, "I shall try very hard to do so. But what about this mistake you speak of. It is in connection with the Spider!"

"Yes. My mistake was in underestimating him as an adversary. I knew that in this operation I would doubtless have the Spider to contend with. But I thought I had planned well and carefully, so as to eliminate that danger. Now I find I must destroy the Spider before going on with my other plans. You, Olga, are going to be the principal means of trapping him for me."

She moved her chair a little closer to the desk. "That will be interesting," she murmured. "Tell me more."

The voice of the hooded man came in muffled tones through his gruesome-appearing headgear. "We know, but the police do not know, that young Frank Dunning, the chauffeur, is secretly engaged to Evelyn Appleton, the daughter of the man he is accused of murdering. We are going to make use of that secret connection to bring the Spider into our little net.

"Leave me now, Olga, and return in an hour. I will have full instructions for you. You can spend that hour in imagining the things that would be done to you, if you should be so indiscreet as to mention anywhere else the name which you spoke a few minutes ago in this room."

Looking at that expressionless black mask which covered the face of the man behind the desk, the woman Olga shuddered. "I—I'll never repeat that name again—even to myself."

The man whom she had addressed as Count Calypsa watched

her without speaking as she arose and crossed the room to the wall at the left. She pulled aside the hanging, revealing a dark paneled wall. She stood there waiting, and the hooded man pressed a button on his desk. Soundlessly a section of the wall slid away, revealing a passageway.

She spoke again, nervously: "Thank you. I will be back in an hour." She stepped through the opening, and the panel slid back once more, leaving the hooded man alone in the room.

He did not remove his mask. Instead he pressed another button on his desk, and the call-o-phone box at his side became illuminated. A voice from the box said: "At your service, sir."

The Dictator's unemotional orders flowed from the slit in his hood with cold efficiency.

"My plans have not been going through as smoothly as they should. At Riverside Drive, where I directed operations personally, I was almost shot. The machine-gunners in the hearse were bunglers. They fired a full minute too soon. Number Ninety-two, who furnished those men, must be punished. You will assign Numbers Thirty-six, Thirty-seven and Thirty-eight, to that task."

"Your order is noted, sir," the voice came through the call-o-phone box.

The hooded man went on: "Commissioner Kirkpatrick is still alive. He must be eliminated at once. You will assign Numbers Fifty, Fifty-one, Fifty-two and Eighty-three to that task."

The voice from the call-o-phone repeated: "Order noted, sir."

"Further, there is now no doubt in my mind that Richard Wentworth is the Spider. He, too, must be eliminated. He has disappeared from his Riverside Drive residence. He has probably assumed the disguise, and I am now at a disadvantage as I cannot put my finger on him. I want him located with the least possible waste of time. You will assign as many men as may be necessary to the task of locating the Spider—even up to a hundred."

"Order noted, sir. The Spider to be located at all costs."

"Operation Number Thirteen, which is planned for tomorrow evening at eight-thirty, must be carried out on schedule."

"But sir, that is the Grand Central Station operation. According to your plans, it will be necessary to control the movements of the police for the successful completion of that operation. If Kirkpatrick remains as commissioner, that will be impossible—"

"That will be taken care of, Number One, before tomorrow night. If your men succeed in eliminating Kirkpatrick, I am thoroughly certain that my own man in the Police Department will be appointed commissioner. But see that you do not fail, or it shall be necessary for me to find another Number One man."

"I will do my best, sir. Do you wish Kirkpatrick killed or—"

"No, I think that since the failure of the Riverside Drive attempt, we will change our method here. The same treatment that we used for Harlan Foote should be employed now."

"Very good, sir. Any further orders?"

"The girl, Evelyn Appleton, the daughter of Howard Appleton, is to be found and put under surveillance at all times. I shall want to arrange a meeting between her and Olga Laminoff sometime during the night."

"Noted, sir."

"Also, the woman, Nita Van Sloan, and the girl, Elaine Robillard, must be placed in custody. If our plans for trapping the

Spider should fail tonight, we will exert pressure upon him through those two. That is all for the present. Sign off."

There was a click, and the light in the call-o-phone box became extinguished. For a long time the hooded man sat in the tall, throne-like chair under the emblem of the lion, and he did not move. Then, arising from his chair, he went to a door in the opposite wall from that through which Olga Laminoff had passed. He pressed his thumbs against two different spots in the wall under the hangings, and another sliding door opened soundlessly. He passed through this, and suddenly the light in the room went out, leaving it in utter darkness.

CHAPTER 4
A JOB WITH FIVE-STAR

A POORLY-DRESSED man shuffled along Broadway, apparently without any definite destination. He wore no overcoat, though the weather was quite cold. His trousers were baggy, and his jacket collar was turned up as a meager protection against the inclement weather.

To the casual observer he might have been a working man come over to Broadway from some squalid residential district to see the bright lights; or he might have been a habitual hanger-on of the Great White Way who was down on his luck. In any case, there was not enough about him to attract a second glance from anyone.

However, a really careful observer might have been impressed by the breadth of this man's shoulders, by the narrow waistline, and by the gleam of keen alertness in his eyes, which was veiled by his general appearance of casualness.

In addition, a close observer might have noticed the two almost imperceptible bulges under this man's armpits.

This shabby man stopped for a moment before one of the many run-down office buildings which offered space to the numerous questionable enterprises that seek to do business along Broadway. His eye rested on one of the brass plates in the directory of occupants. That plate read:

FIVE-STAR DETECTIVE AGENCY
Confidential Investigations Everywhere
Room 511

The shabby man paused before the building for only a moment, then entered. He took the elevator up to the fifth floor, and walked down the corridor until he came to Room 511. At this hour of the evening most of the occupants of the building had gone home. But a number of theatrical agencies were still open, and one or two lights showed on the floor in addition to that in the office of the Five-Star Detective Agency.

The shabby man pushed open the door, and blinked at the flood of light in the main office of the detective agency. Half a dozen girls were busy at desks, transcribing reports. A switchboard operator was busily answering the phone. Behind the general office there was a corridor from which opened the doors of four inner offices. Apparently the Five-Star Detective Agency was a prosperous, busy concern—so busy that it kept going into all hours of the night.

HUGH VARNER

FRANK DUNNING

ARGYLE DUNNING

The shabby man blinked as he approached the switchboard operator, and he asked her: "Can I see the boss, please?"

The girl looked at him quizzically. "Have you an appointment?"

"No. I'm looking for a job."

She hesitated, looked him over carefully, then shrugged and plugged the wire into her switchboard, rang one of the inner offices. She conveyed the message, listened a moment, then with an upward glance said to the visitor: "What's your name?"

"Smith."

The girl raised her eyebrows and repeated the name into the telephone. She listened a moment, then said: "The boss wants to know who sent you."

"Nobody sent me. But I heard around the street that you were hiring extra help."

"I'm sorry, mister, but there

are no jobs open. You came to the wrong place."

Mr. Smith suddenly showed a little aggressiveness. He leaned over the switchboard: "Look here, miss, you better let me talk to your boss. I want a job, see, and I'm going to stay here till I talk to him."

The girl said: "Oh, yeah?" Surreptitiously her finger touched a buzzer at the side of the switchboard. Almost at once a tall, burly man came out from an office at the side, not in the corridor with the private offices.

The visitor had a glimpse for a moment of the room from which the burly man had come. It was filled with smoke, and he could see that there were at least a dozen men seated in the room. THE BURLY man came up to the switchboard, glared at the visitor, and said to the switchboard operator: "Whatsamatter, Mamie?"

MAYOR LARRIBEE

BROCK

CASEY GROGAN

The girl jerked her thumb at Mr. Smith. "It's this guy, Mr. Sorenson. He wants a job, and he won't take no for an answer. Says he will stay here whether we like it or not."

At the name of Sorenson, the shabby man's face seemed to tighten just a trifle. Keen eyes studied the big fellow carefully. Sorenson came up close to the visitor, growled: "Tough guy, huh? You gonna get out of here peaceable, or will you get thrown out?"

Mr. Smith suddenly shed his slouching attitude. He straightened, and amazingly it appeared that he was as tall, if not taller, than Sorenson. The slouch had disappeared from his back, and his voice assumed a hardness that had not been there before. "Listen, you," he rapped, "I came here for a job, and I'm going to talk to the big boss. It will take more than you to throw me out."

Sorenson grinned wickedly. "Just askin' for it, ain't you?" One big hand went into his hip pocket and came out with a leather-thonged blackjack. His other hand reached out to grip the shabby man's coat lapels.

But Mr. Smith suddenly revealed a deadly speed. His left hand caught Sorenson's wrist, and twisted it savagely. Sorenson gasped and dropped the blackjack. In the same instant Mr. Smith's right fist pistoned in a short jab that caught Sorenson squarely in the abdomen and doubled him up, sending him crashing back into the wall.

Sorenson's face purpled with rage as he gasped, trying to catch his breath. Mr. Smith straightened his coat and smiled slightly. "Sorry, Mr. Sorenson, but you asked for it."

The girls in the office had suddenly stopped the clattering of their typewriters, and gasps of surprise went up from all of them.

The switchboard operator was frantically pushing the buzzer alongside her switchboard. The door of the room from which Sorenson had come now opened once more, and men began piling out in answer to the switchboard operator's summons.

Sorenson picked himself up from the floor, cursing, and his hand went for the gun in his shoulder holster. He shouted to the other men who had come rushing into the room: "Hold everything, guys. I'll take this monkey!"

Several of the other men were already drawing guns. But Mr. Smith was in no way overawed by this display of belligerency. Instead, his two hands moved with such lightning speed that it was almost impossible for the eye to follow him. They crossed over his chest, then swung back in almost one continuous motion. In each fist there was a snub-nosed, blue-barreled automatic. Sorenson and the other men froze under the threat of those two deadly guns.

Mr. Smith said mildly: "You'll have to excuse me, gentlemen. I don't like this business of gunplay. But I got to talk to your boss."

Sorenson's hand slowly came away empty from his shoulder holster. His eyes were wide with unbelief. "Gawd!" he muttered. "I never seen a draw like that. Say, you ain't no ordinary punk!"

Mr. Smith smiled. "That's what I've been trying to tell you, Mr. Sorenson. It's—"

He stopped as one of the doors from an inner office opened and a tall man stepped into the outer office. This man, in his late fifties, carried himself with an air of authority. He was Martin Kreamer, the head of the Five-Star Detective Agency.

Kreamer frowned, demanded shortly: "What's going on here?"

Sorenson had already picked himself up from the floor, and he motioned for the other men to retire into the back room. They backed out, throwing respectful glances toward Kreamer.

Sorenson said: "This man says his name is Smith, Mr. Kreamer. He came here looking for a job, and when he got tough I tried to throw him out. But he's got the goods. I never saw a draw as fast as his. Maybe you could use him."

Mr. Smith smiled, and deftly replaced the two automatics in his shoulder holster. "I heard you were hiring men, Mr. Kreamer, so I came up. All I want is a chance to make good."

Martin Kreamer studied him carefully for a moment, then nodded to Sorenson. "All right. I'll talk to him. Come inside."

Mr. Smith eagerly followed Martin Kreamer across the outer office into the inner room. Sorenson did not accompany them. ONCE IN the private office, Kreamer motioned to a chair, and seated himself behind his desk. He lit a cigar without offering one to his visitor, then puffed it slowly, letting his shrewd eyes study every characteristic of his visitor's face and attitude.

Mr. Smith's face was not an extraordinary one. The nose was a little wide, the teeth slightly stained and discolored. The forehead was low, topped by very black hair parted in the center. The eyebrows were very thick, and there were lines around Mr. Smith's mouth. He was apparently somewhere in his late forties.

Of course, Martin Kreamer could not know as he inspected his visitor that the wide nose was caused by two very cleverly constructed platinum plates which had been inserted in the nostrils; that the discolored teeth were really artistic caps carefully mounted upon the man's natural teeth; that the hair had been painstakingly dyed black from the roots out, and that the thick, bushy eyebrows had been artificially superimposed upon Mr. Smith's natural eyebrows.

Stripped of all those disguising touches, the face of Mr. Smith would have become the face of Richard Wentworth, alias the Spider.

But if Martin Kreamer noticed anything unnatural about his visitor's appearance, he gave no sign of it. Instead, after a suitable interval of inspection, he said: "So you want a job?"

Mr. Smith nodded eagerly. "Give me a chance, Mr. Kreamer. I'm a fast man with my fists, and I guess I'm even faster with a gun. I need dough badly, and I'll do anything."

Kreamer said noncommittally: "We're not in the habit of hiring strangers who walk in on us like this. We generally investigate our men carefully. We like to know whom we have working for us. You'll have to tell me more about yourself."

"All right. The name is Jake Smith. I come from Cleveland. I might as well come clean with you. The cops are looking for me."

"What for?"

Smith grinned. "There was a jewelry store that got held up there ten days ago. Maybe you read about it in the papers. The proprietor thought he was a wise guy, and reached for a gun. He got a slug between the eyes."

Martin Kreamer frowned. "You have the nerve to walk in here and tell me that you're wanted for murder? How do you know I won't turn you in to the police?"

Jake Smith did not appear too much disturbed. "I didn't say I had committed murder. I only said there was a jewelry store held up. And besides, I've been hearing that you're taking on a lot of the boys that's on the lam from other cities."

"Where did you hear that?" Kreamer asked crisply.

Smith shrugged. "Oh, here and there. I've been in town a couple of days, and I get around. How about the job?"

Kreamer was looking at him speculatively. "Let's see that draw of yours again—"

"Sure," said Smith. And before the word was out of his mouth his hands had crossed over his chest, and the two automatics were pointing unwaveringly at the detective agency proprietor's chest. Smith smiled tightly.

Kreamer jerked back, startled at the suddenness with which those guns had appeared. The long ash fell from the end of his cigar. "God! Sorenson was right."

Satisfied, Jake Smith holstered his guns once more. "Glad you like it, Mr. Kreamer. Can you use me?"

"I might," Kreamer said reflectively, "be able to use you, at that. I think you're the one man who could meet a certain person that interests us. In a gun fight. You know who I mean?"

Smith shook his head.

"I mean—the Spider."

Smith's eyes narrowed. "You tangling with the Spider?"

Kreamer's eyes were fixed steadily on his visitor. "Would you take a job that would mean your coming up against the Spider in a gun fight?"

"Why not? I never yet met a guy who was faster with a gun than me. This Spider might not be what he's cracked up to be."

Kreamer nodded. "All right. But you'll have to be passed on by somebody besides me. That somebody will check up on you every which way. He'll find out all about your past. If you shape up okay, the job is yours. You'll be paid a hundred dollars a week."

Smith's eyes were gleaming. "Why, that's what I call gold! And only a few minutes ago I almost got chucked out of the office!"

Kreamer leaned forward in his chair. "But there's something else for you to bear in mind. When this party that I speak of checks up on you, if it turns out that you're a phony, *you'll wish to God you had never walked into this office!*"

"I'll take my chances," Smith said flatly.

Kreamer nodded. "Wait a minute while I get the okay on you."

HE PICKED up the phone and dialed a number. While he was doing this, Smith leaned back in his chair and closed his eyes as if he were relaxing. In reality, his mind was sharply alert, and his ears were listening carefully. Each time that Kreamer released the dial indicator, Smith was counting the number of clicks which it took to return to the normal position. To the average ear those dial clicks seemed to merge into one another in one long scraping sound. But to the keen senses of the man who sat in that chair, there were a distinct number of clicks.

Mentally, he tabulated them one after the other: *two, four, three, nine, two, ten, ten.*

Wentworth's alert mind stored that series of figures in his memory. *Two, four, three, nine, two, ten, ten.* He would be able to call those numbers up in his mind when he needed them again. By referring to a telephone dial, he would be able to tell exactly what number Kreamer had just dialed.

Now, he opened his eyes again, seemed to watch lazily, without any special interest as Kreamer talked with his mouth close to the hush-a-phone attachment on the telephone. It was impossible for him to hear what Kreamer was saying. But his blood was racing with excitement. He had spent a whole day ambling around Broadway, going from one underworld retreat to another, having a drink here, another there, mingling in conversations wherever possible. And he had picked up a very meager amount of information.

But among that information was the hint that Martin Kreamer, the head of the Five-Star Detective Agency, was the Number One man for the mysterious Dictator. And here he was, by an incredible stroke of good fortune combined with the skillful playing of the cards as they had fallen, sitting in Kreamer's office while the latter was actually arranging to give him a job in the Dictator's organization.

He knew very well that he was by no means to consider himself an accepted member of that organization. He knew very well that there would be some sort of test as well as a very careful examination of the story he had told. But he had laid the ground carefully. Unless this mysterious Dictator were a man of a much greater degree of intelligence than Wentworth credited him with, he should stand a good chance of getting away with his imposture. He wished that he could listen in on that conversation. The hush-a-phone rendered that impossible, but it would have been very enlightening to him had he been able to hear.

For Kreamer was saying: "This is Number One, sir. I've got a man here who gives the name of Smith. His story sounds a little queer, but he's the fastest man with a pair of guns I've ever seen. I thought maybe we could use him in a pinch if it came to a question of burning down the Spider. I don't think even the Spider could be faster than he is."

From the other end of the phone came the voice of the hooded Dictator: "You must be careful, Number One. Do not forget the possibility that this man may even be the Spider himself, in disguise. Have you thought of that?"

Kreamer restrained a visible start. "I haven't thought of it, sir. But now that you mention it—he's uncannily swift with those guns of his. I imagine that's the way the Spider would be—"

The Dictator chuckled evilly. "Wouldn't it be funny if the Spider walked in on us that way? But I don't think even he would have the gall to try it. Have you got his fingerprints?"

"Yes, sir. I let him open the door of my office when we came in. His prints are on the knob outside, and my men have probably taken them off already. I'll have a report in a short time."

"Good. We'll give this man a chance. If he proves to be bona fide, we can make good use of him. As a first assignment, send him over to the Casey Grogan Dance Hall. There's a bouncer's job vacant there, and I want one of our own men stationed in that place, to make reports of everything that happens. In the meantime, you will check his fingerprints, and I will conduct other investigations about him. Tell him not to take no for an answer, but to make Grogan give him the job by whatever means he can."

Kreamer laughed shortly. "With this guy's guts, I'm sure he'll get the job. Any further orders, sir?"

"No. Report to me as soon as you have found Evelyn Appleton. Sign off now."

KREAMER HUNG up, and smiled at Smith. "Well, you're hired. Now this first assignment is going to be a sort of test. You know where Casey Grogan's Dance Hall is located on Fifty-fourth Street?"

"I think I know that place. You want it shot up?"

"No, no. There's a job as bouncer open over there. You're to go and get that job. Sell yourself to Casey Grogan. Get him to give you the job, and then keep your eyes and ears open. You'll report back here to me whatever happens that might be of interest."

"Such as what?"

Kreamer shrugged. "Oh, you can keep your eye out for any strange characters, or anything like that. After you've been there a day or so I'll give you definite instructions as to what to watch for."

Smith nodded. "I get it. This is just a test. If my—er—references turn out to be okay, then I get a better assignment. Is that it?"

Kreamer smiled twistedly. "That's the idea. Now get going."

Mr. Smith got up, and as Kreamer did not offer to shake

hands, the visitor quietly left the office. In the outside room, Sorenson was waiting for him. Mr. Smith said: "I'm sorry about that jab in the stomach I gave you, Mr. Sorenson."

"Never mind that," the big man growled. "I've been socked harder than that in my life. Did you get the job?"

Smith nodded. "I'm on trial."

"Well," Sorenson told him, "lemme give you a tip. Don't you ever try to pull nothing on Mr. Kreamer or on anyone else in this outfit. It's dangerous."

"Thanks," Mr. Smith said dryly. "I'll remember that."

With narrowed eyes, Sorenson watched him leave the office. The big man shook his head. "I don't like that guy," he said to the switchboard operator. "He's too damn smooth!"

Martin Kreamer came out from the inner office. "Sorenson!" he called. "Did you check on his fingerprints?"

"I took off the knob with his print, and stuck another one on the door. Masters is in the next room now, developing the print."

Just then the door of the operatives room opened, and Masters came in. This was the man who had been Sorenson's partner at the time of the young Dunning's arrest.

Masters' face wore a puzzled frown. He was holding the door-knob which Sorenson had removed from Kreamer's door. It was an old trick, which the Five-Star Agency had often used in the past. All of their doors were equipped with highly sensitized, quickly removable doorknobs, for the purpose of recording the fingerprints of any visitors. In this way many callers who never suspected it had their fingerprints on file in the offices of the Five-Star Detective Agency.

Now, however, something seemed to have gone wrong. Masters was fingering the knob in a puzzled way, and he looked at Sorenson, then asked: "Did this guy wear gloves?"

Sorenson shook his head. "No. I'm sure he didn't. Why?"

Masters still looked puzzled. "Well, he couldn't have touched this doorknob, because there ain't a single fingerprint on it!"

"Impossible!" Martin Kreamer exclaimed. "I was very careful not to touch that knob when I went out, and when we came back in the office I stood aside and let Smith open the door. *I distinctly saw him touch that doorknob, and he did not wear gloves!*"

"Then," Masters exclaimed, "there's something phony here. This doorknob is as clean as a whistle!"

Kreamer barked: "Let me have that knob!" He took it from Masters, examined it carefully, then sniffed at it. His eyes narrowed. His lips pursed into a noiseless whistle. "Smell that!" He thrust the knob into Sorenson's hand.

Sorenson sniffed at it, too, said: "It's got a funny smell—like ether—"

Kreamer swore softly. "Ether is right, Sorenson. That man Smith is deeper than he looks. You know what you smelled on that? That's collodion. He had his fingertips coated with collodion, and they left no print!" Kreamer's voice dropped, and he said very low to Sorenson and Masters: "I think this man Smith is more than he appears to be. You two boys had better get out after him and keep tabs on what he does. Understand?"

"We understand, boss," Sorenson said softly.

"He's going over to Casey Grogan's," Kreamer went on. "Pick him up from there."

"Right," Sorenson said.

The two detectives turned and swiftly went out after the mysterious Mr. Smith.

Kreamer stood in the center of the office, frowning, lost in thought for a moment. Then he hurried back into his private office and dialed a number. As soon as he had his connection, he said: "This is Number One again, sir. This man Smith, sir—I'm afraid there's something phony in that set-up...."

CHAPTER 5
DOOM ON THE WIRE

WHEN RICHARD WENTWORTH, alias the Spider, alias Jake Smith, reached the street from the offices of the Five-Star Detective Agency, Broadway was growing more crowded by the minute. A steady stream of New Yorkers was jostling into the subway kiosk at the corner. Other hundreds were already moving in closely packed throngs up and down Broadway, on their way to dine and dance. Times Square seemed to be a seething mass of hurrying humanity. Barkers for picture shows and burlesque theaters shouted their raucous messages in an endeavor to tempt the passersby to patronize their respective houses.

Wentworth's thoughts were bitter as he scanned all these thousands of people, hurrying home, or to leisurely dinners, heedless of the sinister undercurrents of crime which were threatening to drag men down to their death.

What if these people were suddenly to be informed that a

sinister dictator of the underworld was welding all the criminal elements of the city into a vast organization that would soon strike at their own homes, at their own lives, at their own wives and children? Somewhere in the city this dictator was sitting at this very moment, possibly reviewing his accomplishments of the last few days—the murder of Patrick Sargent, the madness of Harlan Foote, the slaying of Howard Appleton and Phillips Larrabie. Perhaps he was chuckling at the thought of young Frank Dunning in the clutches of the law, accused of the murder of his employer. Perhaps this dictator was planning the next great step in his campaign for power. What would that step be?

Wentworth tried to put himself in the place of this mysterious master of the underworld. Where would he logically strike next? Larrabie had guessed that Wentworth was the Spider; would it not therefore be logical that this dictator should also have guessed the same thing? Would he attempt to strike at Wentworth through those whom Wentworth loved—Nita, or Elaine Robillard? Or would he attempt to follow up his efforts to eliminate Kirkpatrick?

Wentworth moved north on Broadway toward Casey Grogan's Dance Hall. He tried to isolate in his mind a name that might identify the dictator. For this dictator must be someone well known in the city—someone with many connections, enabling him to operate in this fashion. He must be someone who was ruthless, clever, cruel, and powerful enough to command the obedience of an unscrupulous man like Martin Kreamer.

Hugh Varner, the banking attorney, and Stephen Pelton,

the City Comptroller, had both given false testimony which tended to incriminate young Frank Dunning. That false testimony might be the result of honest mistakes in observation on their part: yet, on the other hand, it might have been deliberately done. In the latter case, both Varner and Pelton must come under suspicion. Both wielded great influence, both were clever men, and they were both ambitious. It would not be difficult to imagine either Varner or Pelton as aspiring to attain the power which a dictator of the underworld could command.

Inspector Strong, Wentworth was certain, was not of a caliber to be the guiding force behind this movement. Wentworth knew that Strong had been appointed Inspector of Homicide from the outside, over the heads of dozens of other deserving officers. Kirkpatrick would never keep him. And if Strong was a tool of the Dictator, then it would become imperative for the Dictator to remove Kirkpatrick. Wentworth felt that his friend, the commissioner, was in imminent danger. But Kirkpatrick was warned, and would see to it that he was well guarded.

The Spider stopped at Fifty-fourth Street and bought an evening newspaper, scanned the headlines. The main story of the day, spread across the whole front page, gave him food for thought:

ARGYLE DUNNING BECOMES MAYOR

At a special ceremony this afternoon, Argyle Dunning, President of the Board of Aldermen, was sworn in before Chief Justice Murray as Mayor of this city to succeed Phillips Larrabie, who was assassinated last night. Mayor Dunning announced he would appoint a new police commissioner, but there is some question as to whether his authority permits him to revoke Mayor Larrabie's appointment of Commissioner Kirkpatrick.

Argyle Dunning's nephew, Frank Dunning, is still being held in the Tombs pending trial on the charge of murdering his employer, Howard Appleton. Mayor Dunning announced that young Frank Dunning, his nephew, would receive no special consideration as the nephew of the Mayor. The chauffeur will have to stand trial as if he were an average citizen...."

Wentworth folded the paper and stuffed it in his pocket, then continued east on Fifty-fourth Street toward the tall neon sign in the middle of the block which read:

CASEY GROGAN'S DANCE HALL

He walked slowly, because his mind was struggling with a problem—the problem of just where Argyle Dunning stood in the situation. As President of the Board of Aldermen, Argyle Dunning was the person to benefit most directly by the death of Phillips Larrabie, for he automatically became mayor.

On the other hand, it was unreasonable to suppose that a man would deliberately frame his own nephew for murder. And since it was logical to assume that the same hand was behind the murders of both Larrabie and Appleton, one would have to believe that if Argyle Dunning was responsible for Larrabie's death, he was also responsible for having placed his nephew in jail as the accused murderer of Howard Appleton.

Whoever this Dictator was, he had been clever enough to so confuse the situation, to so befuddle the issues, that it would be almost impossible to point the finger of suspicion at any one man as the result of a logical course of reasoning. For that, Wentworth's respect for this unknown Dictator increased tremendously.

The Spider still remembered that series of numbers he had memorized in Kreamer's office. He repeated them now as he walked: *two, four, three, nine, two, ten, ten.* He did not delude himself into the belief that by merely checking these numbers back on the dial phone he could trace the mysterious Dictator whom Kreamer served. That would be expecting too much stupidity from a man who had shown himself so clever thus far. There would be some blind connection there along the line— some break in the back trail to the Dictator; for the unknown ruler of the underworld would not make it that easy for his Number One man to search him out. Nevertheless, it would afford an avenue of investigation if all else failed.

WENTWORTH HAD arrived in front of Casey Grogan's dance hall now, and he abruptly put all speculation behind him. Once more he was Jake Smith, the fugitive killer, trying to make good on an assignment given him by the Dictator's Number One man. His keen eyes glanced up and down the street, sizing it up out of force of habit.

He saw a taxicab pull up across the street, and momentarily the faces of the two men within it were illuminated by a street lamp. Then the taxi moved on a few feet before stopping, and the faces were thrown in darkness again. But that moment had been sufficient. Wentworth recognized Sorenson and Masters. He smiled to himself.

That doorknob trick back at the Five-Star's offices had not been lost on him. Kreamer was very clever—clever enough to have caught the scent of collodion on that doorknob. His suspicions had been aroused, and he had sent Sorenson and Masters to check up. Well, he would give them no grounds for suspicion. The fact that he had used collodion on his fingertips would not of itself damn him in the eyes of the Dictator's organization; rather, it should recommend him to the Dictator as one worthy of promotion in the organization.

Wentworth gave no sign that he had recognized the two men in the cab. He walked under the wide, brilliantly illuminated marquee of the dance hall, stepped past the doorman and the hat-check girl without surrendering his hat, and went up the flight of stairs which led to the dance hall.

This was a cheap, old, rundown building. It had at one time been used as a manufacturers' showroom and warehouse; but the neighborhood had deteriorated, and this building had long been unoccupied. Some six months ago Casey Grogan, an ex-prize-fighter, had leased the building and renovated two floors at great expense. He had hired two bands, put in a bar, and set about a hundred girls to work as dancing partners. Men in search of fun could come here and buy a strip of tickets at ten cents each. These tickets entitled them to dance with one of the "hostesses" at the rate of one ticket per dance.

The income of the place was greatly increased by the bar, as each hostess received a commission on the amount of money her customer spent on drinks. The upper of the two floors was devoted to what Grogan called private dance studios, where one could learn to dance at moderate cost, under the instruction of attractive young women. All in all, Casey made a good living out of the dance hall, though it did not run into a fortune.

There was a good deal of speculation as to where he got the money to equip the dance hall. He had not been widely known in the boxing world prior to his venture into this business. He had appeared in a few preliminary bouts in the Middle West, and then had graduated to the semifinal class, but he had never really reached the top. Some said that he had made his money by running arms into South America, while others said that he had won it at the race track. Wherever it came from, he was now running a semi-legitimate business which, though frowned on by reformers, was tolerated by the police. Wentworth wondered as to the cause of the Dictator's interest in knowing what was going on in a place of this type.

When he reached the top of the stairs he did not enter the dance hall proper, but passed by the two ticket booths where one bought dance tickets, and made his way through the bar, which was fairly well crowded. At the rear of the bar were two doors. One was marked "Office of the Manager," and the other was marked "Office of Mr. Grogan."

Wentworth knocked at this latter door, and a gruff voice from inside called out: "Come on in. What are you waiting for?"

Wentworth smiled, pushed open the door and entered. Casey Grogan was sitting at a battered old desk facing the door. He was a well-built man with a long head and lively, intelligent eyes. His face was that of a battered prizefighter. His nose was twisted, giving evidence of having been broken in at least two places. His left ear was bunched and gnarled, and his lips were thick. There was a scar over his right eye, and another over his temple. He looked up as Wentworth closed the door behind him, then frowned.

"I thought you was Krauss, my manager. What the hell do you want?"

In spite of the gruffness of his tone, there was a lively, boyish curiosity in the way he spoke, and in the look on his face.

Wentworth smiled and said: "I hear you got a job open, Mr. Grogan. A job as bouncer. I'd like to get it."

"What's your name?"

"Jake Smith. I'm from Cleveland. I could handle the job for you swell, Mr. Grogan. I'm handy with my dukes, and I can take care of any trouble."

"Hmm," said Grogan, musingly. He looked Jake Smith up and down appraisingly. "You look like a good hefty guy. Who told you about the job?"

"Martin Kreamer, over at the Five-Star Agency—"

"Is that so!" Grogan roared. "So Kreamer told you about it, did he? Well, you scram to hell out of here and go back and tell that skunk of a Kreamer I won't have nothin' to do with any of his crew!" Grogan pulled open a drawer of his desk and snatched out a revolver. "I know all about Kreamer. Now you get to hell out of here before I shoot you full of holes—"

He stopped, open-mouthed, the revolver still half out of the drawer. He was staring straight into the twin black holes of Wentworth's two automatics, which had appeared miraculously as if by some unexplainable legerdemain.

"Hold everything, Mr. Grogan!" Wentworth said. "You got me all wrong. I came to this town looking for a job, and I ribbed Kreamer first because I heard he was hiring a lot of men. I don't know him from a hole in the wall. He sent me here. Now if you got anything against Kreamer, don't hold it against me. I need a job bad, and you got one open. Why can't we get together?"

SLOWLY, AS if fascinated by those two unwavering gun muzzles, Grogan replaced the revolver in the drawer. Then he sighed deeply, and leaned back in his chair. He wiped a trace of perspiration from his forehead.

"L-listen," he gasped, "did you really pull those guns outta your pocket? I never even seen your hands move."

The spurious Mr. Jake Smith smiled and holstered the automatics. "I guess I'm pretty fast with a roscoe," he said modestly.

"I guess you are," Grogan said earnestly. He got up and came around the desk. Wentworth noted that his body was amazingly supple, and he walked with the grace of one who was accustomed to handling himself fast in the ring. Grogan said: "If you're as fast with your dukes as you are with a gun, the job is yours. Let's try you out. Put 'em up."

He squared off, and Jake Smith grinned, put up his fists. Grogan said: "Don't pull your punches. This ain't foolin'. When I try a guy out, I try him out—what I mean."

Grogan feinted with his left, came in hard with a right. Jake Smith moved his head barely an inch, and Grogan's huge right fist whistled harmlessly through the air. Wentworth had studied boxing under greater masters than Grogan would ever know;

and though Grogan was a professional, Wentworth knew at once that he could take the man's measure.

He allowed the boxer to try for another swift knockout, dodged that one, then stepped in, his right and left pistoning with the timed precision of a powerful machine. His fists sank into Grogan's stomach mercilessly in quick alternate blows that gave the man no chance to defend himself.

Grogan backed away, covering up feebly. He sidestepped, attempted to land a blow below Wentworth's belt. But Wentworth saw it coming, watched him, and sent a left to the side of his jaw that rocked Grogan's head. Grogan jumped backward, and yelled: "Hey! That's enough!"

Wentworth dropped his hands and stepped back, smiling. Grogan leaned against the wall for a minute, shook his head to clear it, then exclaimed: "Whew! You got what it takes, guy. The job is yours." Grogan grinned. "If I could fight like you can fight, guy, I'd still be in the ring—instead of running a joint like this!"

He went back to his chair behind the desk. "I pay thirty-five a week. Any drinks you have at the bar you got to pay for out of your own pocket. Your job is just to hang around in case of emergency. You dance with the girls, just like a regular customer, and you float around the place and in and out from the bar.

"There's a buzzer in the hall and one on the dance floor and one in the bar. One ring means trouble in the barroom, two rings mean trouble on the dance floor, three rings mean trouble upstairs in the dance studio.

"Wherever there's trouble, that's where you earn your dough. It's your job to grab those troublemakers and take 'em apart and see what makes 'em tick, and then kick 'em out on their ear. You got to treat 'em rough, so they won't want to come back. Get the idea?"

"I get it," Jake Smith said. "When do I start?"

"You can start tonight, if you're ready. It's early. You come to work about half-past eight, and you stay on the job till three-thirty, when we close."

Grogan was looking him over closely. "I wonder what a guy like you wants with a cheap job like this." Suddenly his eyes narrowed in suspicion. "Listen, if you showed Kreamer what you showed me, that guy would put you on at a hundred a week. How come he didn't give you a job?"

"I had a scrap with a guy named Sorenson in there," Wentworth told him noncommittally. "I smacked him around a little, and I guess Sorenson is sore at me."

Wentworth had told him nothing but the truth.

Grogan's eyes lit up with amusement. "So you mussed up Sorenson, huh? You should have broke that big baboon's neck. If you ever see him or his sidekick Masters in here, you pick them up by the seat of their pants and chuck them out. Understand?"

"I understand."

Grogan nodded. "Okay. You be back here by eight-thirty. And be ready to work."

Jake Smith said: "Thanks, Grogan. I'll be here."

He left Grogan in the office, and made his way out past the dance floor. There were a few men in the barroom, but only half a dozen couples on the dance floor. Places of this type did not begin to do any amount of business until the very late hours of the night.

AS HE had gone through the barroom, Wentworth had glanced around keenly to see if Sorenson or Masters had come in after him. He saw neither of them, but he also failed to see the face of the man who was talking to the head bartender.

This man had followed Wentworth all the way down Broadway to the building where the office of the Five-Star Detective Agency was located; and he had then followed him back to Casey Grogan's Dance Hall. Now, as Wentworth disappeared, the man raised his head. Had Wentworth looked back he would have recognized his chauffeur, Jackson!

Jackson had come in after Wentworth, and when Wentworth had gone into Grogan's private office, the chauffeur had lounged over toward the door and leaned nonchalantly against it. The sound of voices had come to him through the office door, and he understood that Wentworth was getting a job here. While he had been listening, he also noted that there was only one bartender on duty. So when he was sure that Wentworth was getting the job, Jackson had approached the bartender and asked him if he needed help. It was while Jackson was talking to the bartender that Wentworth had passed through.

Now, the bartender was saying: "We can use a good man here. We're a little short-handed. Put on an apron and let's see if you can mix them."

Jackson had often assisted Jenkyns in mixing drinks at Wentworth's home. There was nothing in the way of fancy concoctions that he could not make. So he gladly took off his coat, put on the apron that the bartender gave him, and stepped behind the bar. At that moment, Krauss, the manager of the place, came in from the dance hall. The bartender called him over, and introduced Jackson.

Krauss was a short, stubby man, with an entirely bald head. He watched carefully while Jackson made in quick succession a side car, a Bacardi, a Tom Collins and an old-fashioned.

The bartender watched with grudging approval. "Say," he exclaimed, "that's fast, clean work. Where'd you pick it up?"

"Here and there," grinned Jackson. To Krauss he said, "How about it?"

Krauss nodded. "You're pretty good. Have you got your union card with you?"

"I have it at home," Jackson lied. "You want me to go back and get it now, or will tomorrow be all right?"

"That's all right," Krauss told him. "You can bring it tomorrow. Start right in now." He explained that the other bartender had not had a day off all week, and that he would go off now since Jackson was capable of taking charge.

Jackson said: "Just give me a chance to make a telephone call, and I'll go to work. I want to tell the wife I won't be home."

"You can use the phone right here," Krauss told him, pointing to the instrument behind the bar.

Jackson thanked him, and picked up the phone. Krauss left, and went into the office of Casey Grogan. "I've just hired a bartender," he told Grogan. "He's making a telephone call. You want to kind of check on him?"

Grogan nodded, picked up the phone and threw in a switch

which connected him with the extension upon which Jackson was talking. He caught Jackson's voice in the middle of a sentence:

"I've got a job here, Miss Nita, and I'll be able to keep an eye on the boss. He—"

Nita's voice came back sharply on the phone: "Be careful, Jackson. Someone may be listening in!"

"All right, Miss. I'll call you again when I go off duty."

Krauss had been holding his ear close to the receiver so that he could hear as well as Grogan. Now as they caught the click of Jackson's phone being hung up, Grogan and Krauss exchanged glances.

"That's damn interesting!" Grogan said softly.

"*Very* interesting," Krauss said. "I thought that guy was too good for an ordinary bartender. What do you think we ought to do with him?"

Grogan was thoughtful. "He'll keep for awhile. He's a spy of some kind, and we've got to find out what it's all about. Trace that call he made, if you can, and then we'll go to work on him after we close."

He got up from behind his desk. "I'm going out now. You can handle everything here. I'll be back around eleven o'clock. Don't let that guy go away."

He got his hat and coat and left through a rear entrance in the office.

Krauss was thoughtful as he came out into the barroom again. He stood there for awhile, watching Jackson deftly serve the customers at the bar. There was a strange gleam in the eyes of the dance hall manager. He strolled into the dance floor, and checked in a number of the girls who were reporting for work. He looked in once more to make sure that Jackson was still on the job, then went downstairs into the lobby and entered one of the telephone booths there. He inserted a coin in the machine, and dialed a number.

When he got his connection he said:

"This is Number Sixty-nine talking. I got a report to make. There's a guy came here and got a job as bartender just now. Right after that he called up a dame named Miss Nita. This guy is too good to be an ordinary bartender. There's something phony about him. You want I should do anything about it, sir?"

The voice of the man at the other end was the disguised voice of the hooded Dictator. "What does this man look like?"

"He's a guy about thirty-five, sir. He's dark-haired, and well built. About five feet seven, and he weighs about one-sixty."

"Well, that can't be the Spider."

Krauss' voice sounded a bit startled. "The Spider! Say, boss, are you after that guy?"

"Never mind what I'm after!" the Dictator rapped out. "I don't like people who ask me questions. Do you understand?"

"Oh, sure, boss, I didn't mean a thing. I just wanted to help. I wouldn't think of askin'—"

"All right. Remember it in the future. Now about this man—does Grogan suspect he's not what he pretends to be?"

"Yes, sir. Grogan listened in with me on the telephone conversation. I couldn't help it."

"All right. Pay no further attention to this man. I will have the matter looked into myself. I am sending a lady named Olga Laminoff to investigate him. You will assist her in any way you can."

"All right, sir. I'll take care of her."

"Very well. Sign off now. If there are any further developments before Olga Laminoff arrives, call me again."

Krauss hung up and went upstairs again. He was very well satisfied with himself. He looked into the barroom again, and grinned as he saw Jackson at work.

"You poor sap," he whispered. "If you knew what was coming your way tonight, you'd jump outta the window."

CHAPTER 6
CALLING THE SPIDER!

WHEN THE Spider left Casey Grogan, he moved swiftly, for he had much to accomplish in the two hours before he was scheduled to return. First he stepped into a drug store, entered a telephone booth, and wrote down on a slip of paper the series of seven numbers he had memorized from Kreamer's office. *Two, four, three, nine, two, ten, ten.*

Two clicks of the dial meant that the second circle had been signaled. That would be A, B, or C. Four clicks on the dial meant that the fourth circle had been signaled. That would be G, H, or I. Three clicks meant that the third circle had been signaled again. Since the third circle represented a number and not a letter, the only thing that could stand for would be 3.

He therefore had an exchange which began with A, B, or C,

and whose second letter was G, H, or I, with a Number 3 following. The only exchange that could be was CHester 3. From there on it was easy. The *nine, two, ten, ten* represented 9200 on the dial. He had his number—CHester 3, 9200.

Swiftly he inserted a coin in the coin box, and asked for the telephone business office. The telephone company made it a rule never to give the name of a subscriber at any particular number. But Wentworth knew how to get it.

"This," he said, "is Special Agent Lawrence of the United States Treasury Department, Badge Number Eighty-three. It is vitally important that I have at once the name and address of the subscriber to Chester three-nine-two-zero-zero."

He was wired through to the Night Investigation Department, and once more gave the name of Special Agent Lawrence, Badge 83. As Richard Wentworth, he knew Lawrence well, and knew also that Lawrence would not object to his use of the name and badge number. In less than three minutes he had the name and address of the subscriber.

And his eyes narrowed calculatingly as he jotted it down. It was—

Hugh Varner, Electrical Building, Forty-second Street.

Wentworth had not expected to find it so easy. That Hugh Varner, the clever attorney for a large banking syndicate, should be the Dictator was not beyond the bounds of possibility; but that he should have been so careless as to permit his Number One man to know who he was, indicated he was so sure of his power that he didn't mind his identity being discovered.

But it didn't jibe with the hooded figure that Wentworth had

Wishard fell to the sidewalk, screaming his voice cutting shrill above the gunfire.

seen on the murder hearse. The discovery that the telephone was listed under Varner's name made the problem more difficult rather than more simple. Wentworth wished now that he had not cut himself off from his friends. Formerly he had been able to command the services of Ram Singh and of Jackson as well as of Nita. He could have sent one of them to investigate that telephone. Now he must plan all his activities with a view to doing everything himself.

He decided with a shrug that he should not follow up the clue of the telephone number at present. Leaving the telephone booth, he stopped at the soda counter for a sandwich and a cup of coffee. He had not eaten since early in the morning. Though he could have gone for another similar period without food, he seized this opportunity to fortify himself while reminded of the necessity. Wentworth's mind, when he was working on a case, operated with such concentrated efficiency that all his physical wants were forgotten.

While he was eating the sandwich the radio behind the counter was blaring forth the program of a popular comedian. That program ended, and a new broadcast followed. Wentworth tensed as the new announcer spoke:

"Tonight, my friends, events here in the city overshadow national and international news. The city seems to be in the grip of the most daring and ruthless criminal organization which it has ever known. One after another, three Commissioners of Police appointed by Mayor Larrabie have met with death or with madness. Mayor Larrabie himself has been killed. Argyle

Dunning, the new mayor, appears to be entirely helpless to cope with the situation.

"Commissioner Kirkpatrick, the last man appointed by Mayor Larrabie, seemed to be doing a good job, but Mayor Dunning has asked him to resign. Kirkpatrick has refused, and there now exists the peculiar situation of a police department with two commissioners. The police are demoralized, and in no position to cope with the criminal elements who are running amuck."

The announcer's voice halted for a moment, and then came again over the radio, tinged with excitement.

"*Flash!* Late bulletin! The Pandora Theatre on Broadway has just been held up by a gang of armed men using submachine guns and tear-gas bombs. The entire receipts of last night and this afternoon, totaling eighteen thousand dollars, were taken. The gangsters fired three bursts from submachine guns into the crowd of patrons who had rushed into the lobby in a panic. They then used the tear-gas guns to effect their escape. Thirty people were killed and nine seriously wounded. For some reason there were no police radio cars in the vicinity to give chase, and the bandits escaped without interference! That is all we know now. As soon as further bulletins arrive we will broadcast them."

WENTWORTH FINISHED his sandwich quickly. The announcer went on:

"It becomes more and more apparent that there is a giant intellect at the head of the criminal underworld once more. The rumors of a Dictator of the underworld are becoming substantiated. Never before has a criminal band engineered a holdup in the heart of Times Square in such a bloodthirsty manner, and escaped—

"*Flash!* Police, when questioned as to why there were no radio cars available, stated that orders had come in from Mayor Dunning to concentrate all radio cars in Manhattan around the Brooklyn Bridge sector, as he explained he had received information that a holdup would take place there. So far that move seems to have accomplished nothing except to facilitate the escape of the Pandora Theatre holdup men.

"Commissioner Kirkpatrick protested vigorously, but Mayor Dunning informed him that he was no longer commissioner. A very difficult legal problem has arisen. When is a commissioner not a commissioner? Mayor Dunning has taken over control of the police department himself, and has demanded Commissioner KirkPatrick's resignation. But since Kirkpatrick has refused to resign, he remains technically the head of the department. The hunt for the criminals is being hampered by the fact that contradictory orders are being issued by Kirkpatrick and by Dunning. It would seem that the Dictator of the underworld has been successful in entirely disrupting our police force. The city is now at his mercy."

There was more to the announcement, but Wentworth did not wait to hear the rest of it. He paid for his sandwich and went out. Down at the middle of the block he could see the large neon sign of Casey Grogan's Dance Hall. He looked carefully for Sorenson and Masters, but could not see them.

A man was standing in a doorway across the street, and Wentworth's eyes narrowed. If he were being followed, he wanted to know it.

He started around the corner up Broadway, and stopped to buy a newspaper. The Pandora Theatre robbery had not yet reached the street, but this edition of the paper contained the story of how the Spider had invaded Police Headquarters and left a warning note for Inspector Strong. There was an editorial in the first column demanding that Mayor Argyle Dunning retain Kirkpatrick as commissioner.

"Kirkpatrick," said the editorial, "has experience, as well as the respect of every honest policeman in the department. If anyone can cope with this new menace that has arisen to bleed the city, it is Commissioner Stanley Kirkpatrick. In the interest of justice and good government we demand that Mayor Dunning retain Kirkpatrick in his position!"

Wentworth skipped the rest of the editorial and let his eyes stray to a box item at the top of the page. He had not noticed it before, because he had had the paper folded over to the first column. Now, the heading struck his eye with the force of a blow:

EVELYN APPLETON APPEALS TO THE SPIDER!

The daughter of Howard Appleton, who was murdered yesterday, believes that Frank Dunning is innocent of her father's killing. She disclosed to reporters for this paper that she has been secretly engaged to Frank Dunning for three weeks. All day she has been striving frantically to obtain help for her fiancé. She visited the City Hall this afternoon in an effort to see Mayor Argyle Dunning, her fiancé's uncle. Mayor Dunning refused to see her. Back at the Tombs where she visited Frank Dunning, she issued the following appeal to a man of whom we have all heard but whom nobody knows:

"I wish to thank the Spider for his faith in Frank. I appreciate the risk that he took in sending the note to Inspector Strong. If the Spider is still interested in helping Frank Dunning to clear himself, I beg that he will get in touch with me in some way. I shall be here at the Tombs all night. No one can make me go home. I shall stay here until Frank is released. Spider, I beg you—do something to help Frank, or they will railroad him to the chair. I have important information to give you if you can get in touch with me. I will go anywhere, or do anything you tell me. For God's sake, help us."

Wentworth's eyes were warm as he read that urgent appeal from a girl in love. He knew how she felt, how frantic, desperate she must be. If he himself were in the same position he knew that Nita would feel that way too—with perhaps the difference that Nita would not be as helpless as Evelyn Appleton was. Swiftly, Wentworth's mind went over the possibilities. Evelyn Appleton had said in her appeal that she had information of importance to impart to him if he could get in touch with her. But why had she chosen to remain at the Tombs? She must know that it would be difficult for him to contact her there. For a moment he wondered if this might not be some trap of the Dictator's. Why should Evelyn Appleton have chosen to appeal to him instead of going to Kirkpatrick, whom everyone knew to be honest and efficient?

Wentworth decided to take the chance.

BUT HE could not go as Jake Smith. He would have to change his identity. For that purpose it would be necessary for him to go to his present headquarters on Sixty-sixth Street. He had a furnished room there under the name of John Worth.

He had had this room for many years, holding it always under this name, keeping it stocked with change of clothes and material for changing his appearance. It was an evidence of his foresight, and it enabled him now to operate without the necessity of getting in touch with his home or with Nita or the others.

But first it would be necessary to make sure that he was not being shadowed.

He walked north on Broadway, and stopped in the middle of the block before an automobile showroom. He looked in through the window at the glittering display of cars just received from the factory.

After a moment or two, he threw a glance backward, and saw the figure of a man turning the corner. He could not see the man's face, but he recognized a tall, well-knit figure. It was the same man. The trailer was careful to keep his face away from the electric light, but Wentworth could note that it was clean-shaven. There was something familiar about this trailer's manner of walking, but the momentary glimpse of the swarthy face, almost black-skinned, gave Wentworth no identification.

The Spider frowned thoughtfully. Somewhere, at some time, he had met that man, he was sure. He turned and walked slowly up the street, and when he reached the corner he crossed to the east side of Broadway. The man who was following him was clever enough not to cross after him, but continued on up Broadway, keeping close to the building line and away from the streetlamp.

Wentworth walked east on Sixty-sixth Street, without looking back. He was puzzled by this shadow. If the man had been placed on his trail by Kreamer, he must at all costs not appear to notice him. It was possible that Sorenson and Masters had left this fellow to trail him. He must give the man the slip in such fashion as not to arouse his shadow's suspicions. He kept on walking without looking back, and at Fifth Avenue he leaped aboard a southbound bus which was just starting with the changing lights.

Climbing to the top, and saw his follower boarding the bus behind.

At Sixty-second Street he ran down the steps of the bus, leaped off, and walked quickly west once more. He saw the second bus pass without stopping, and the man who was trailing him did not get off. Wentworth nodded to himself in satisfaction, and hailed a taxicab, drove to the corner of Sixty-sixth Street and Broadway. He glanced back frequently to make sure that be was not being followed now. He had given his shadower the slip. The man had not expected him to leave the bus so soon. He paid off the taxi, and walked west on Sixty-sixth Street, stopping to tie his shoelace and steal a glance backward. No shadow in sight. He quickly turned into the brownstone-front house where he had his furnished room. He let himself in with his key, mounted the flight of steps to the second floor, and entered his room.

He made sure that the door was locked and the shade down, then drew out his suitcase of makeup material and quickly altered his face, rendering it a little older and more dignified in expression. He had now become, to all outward appearances, a dignified business man of about forty-five. He discarded his shabby suit and donned a well-pressed blue serge suit from the closet. He then picked a gray fedora hat, an ivory-knobbed walking stick, and a briefcase. From a compartment in his valise he extracted a small box containing business cards bearing different names. Out of these cards he selected one with the name of Mark Hawley, Attorney and Counselor-at-law.

Now he was going to try to see Evelyn Appleton.

Into the briefcase he stuck the cape and hat of the Spider. He expected to have use for that outfit before the night was over.

He descended the steps to the ground floor very carefully, and looked out through the ground-glass panel of the front door. A dismayed exclamation broke from his lips as he discerned the figure of a man across the street from the boarding house—the same man who had followed him on the bus. The chap was still careful not to show his face, but Wentworth knew him by the way his coat hung, and by his physique.

Wentworth had been positive that he had given this fellow the slip on Fifth Avenue. He could not guess how the man had managed to pick up his trail again.

Now he boldly stepped out through the front door. His present disguise would be sufficient to carry him past the watcher. No one could connect this dignified, stately-looking business man with the shabby Jake Smith.

Wentworth walked boldly east to Broadway without looking around. At the corner he hailed a taxicab and told the driver: "Tombs Prison."

As the cab moved down Broadway, Wentworth glanced out the window and was startled to see his trailer boarding another taxicab immediately behind him. The man had pierced his disguise!

Suddenly, Wentworth felt a deep hopelessness within him. If this unknown who was following him was working for the Dictator, then his every step for the last couple of days must be known to the mysterious master of the underworld. And it spoke well for the cleverness of the Dictator's henchmen that this trailer had been able to follow him so persistently, and to pierce his disguise. What then would be his chances of check-mating an antagonist who was so well served?

Grimly, Wentworth faced forward in the cab. He would have to take care of that shadower somehow, before the man could report to headquarters.

For if the Dictator learned that Mark Hawley, the attorney, and Jake Smith, the gunman, were one and the same person, Jake Smith would meet short shrift when he returned to duty at Casey Grogan's Dance Hall....

CHAPTER 7
THE TRAP AT THE TOMBS

A S WENTWORTH'S cab passed Fourteenth Street, he saw ahead of him, on the west side of the street, the undertaking establishment of Nicholas Wishard. Wishard had been the head of a large bootleg ring during Prohibition days. With the going of Prohibition, Wishard had sought another business and had purchased this undertaking establishment. But his reputation had not changed. He was known in the underworld as one who could be relied upon to supply weapons and getaway cars to criminals. The undertaking business was merely a front for his other activities.

In sudden inspiration, Wentworth snapped his fingers. That hearse, which had figured in the killing of Mayor Larrabie—the police had not yet been able to identify it, for the motor number and serial numbers had been eradicated, and the license plates were stolen. What if Wishard had supplied that hearse?

As they passed the undertaking establishment, Wentworth saw that there was a light in the place, far in the rear where the office was located. He also noted that a sedan with four men was parked at the curb. His single glimpse of the tense faces of those four men told him that they were not parked there for any idle purpose; for two of them were Sorenson and Masters.

Quickly he tapped on the glass separating him from the driver, and ordered the man to pull in to the curb. He got out, told the cabby to wait.

He noted that the cab with his shadower had passed them, and had also pulled in at the curb farther down the block. He shrugged. Let his trailer follow him now. He didn't care. This was too hot a lead to ignore.

He started back toward the Wishard establishment, and just at that moment he saw that the light in the undertaking parlor was put out. The tall, stoop-shouldered figure of Nicholas Wishard appeared, and the man turned his back to the street as he shut and locked the door.

At the same time, the doors of the sedan at the curb were thrown open, and Masters, Sorenson and the other two men stepped out, each of them holding a revolver.

Richard Wentworth was less than thirty feet away, and he distinctly heard Sorenson call out to Wishard: "Sorry, Wishard, this is by order of the big boss!"

Wishard whirled about, saw them for the first time, and screamed: "Don't! Don't shoot!"

Masters, standing next to Sorenson, mocked him: "Can't take it, huh?"

"Wait!" Wishard yelled. "I can square everything with the Dictator. It wasn't my fault those guys flopped—"

He stopped talking, and his voice fairly rose into a scream of terror as the four guns were raised to a level with his chest.

Wentworth was running now, and he had dropped his briefcase and cane. His hands crossed over his chest, came out with

NITA VAN SLOAN

the two automatics, and the guns spurted twin jets of flame in the direction of the four men.

Masters dropped with the first shot, as did another of the four. Sorenson and the fourth man fired at Wishard three times quickly, and Wishard fell to the ground, screaming, his voice cutting shrilly above the deep-toned reverberations of the gunfire. Wentworth cursed, fired again, and Sorenson's companion fell. Sorenson himself dropped to one knee, aimed at Wentworth.

And Wentworth in that instant heard gunfire behind him!

He knew that the man who had trailed him must be shooting. But strangely, the shadower was not firing at him, for the bullets whined past well to his right, and thudded into the body of Sorenson before the big detective could shoot. Sorenson was hurled backward to the sidewalk, dead almost before he dropped.

Wentworth, puzzled, swung around and almost collided with the trailer who had just killed Sorenson. The two stood stock still, staring at each other. Wentworth slowly lowered his two automatics. A slow smile appeared on his face.

"Well!" he exclaimed. "Was it you all the time, Ram Singh?"

The man who stood there now, the man who had trailed him all the way from Casey Grogan's Dance Hall, was none other than Ram Singh—without his beard.

Ram Singh lowered his head. "It was I, Master. Jackson and I have been trying to watch over you since you left. It was the *memsahib's* order. I—I even made myself unworthy of my race by shaving off my beard the better to follow you."

Wentworth pressed Ram Singh's hand hard. "It was against my orders, but I appreciate it, Ram Singh. Come now, quickly, before a crowd gathers."

HE RAN swiftly toward the doorway of the undertaking establishment. Sorenson, Masters and the other two gunmen were dead. But Wishard still breathed feebly.

Wentworth raised his head. "Wishard! Why did these men shoot you? Why did the Dictator order you killed?"

Wishard was bleeding through the nose. "I'm dying," he

murmured. "I—I was Number Ninety-two in the Dictator's organization. He—he thought I had laid a trap for him. Damn him, he kills everybody who fails!"

Wentworth bent closer. "You're dying, Wishard. The Dictator ordered you killed. You hate him. Tell me who he is and I'll get him for you."

"God help me," Wishard groaned, "I don't know—who he is. But—" A horrible laugh mingled with the bloody gurgling from his throat—"I'll even up with him. I know something. He's planning—a big operation of the gang—at Grand Central Station—*tonight at twelve.* Whoever you are—be there—with plenty of help. Get the Dic—"

His voice died to a whisper, and the last words faded into nothingness.

"What sort of operation is he planning?" Wentworth demanded.

Wishard mumbled: "Holdup tonight at—"

Suddenly Wishard's jaw fell open slackly, and his eyes glazed. He became limp in Wentworth's arms.

The Spider lowered his head to the ground, stood up. A crowd had gathered, but was keeping its distance. Somewhere a policeman was blowing his whistle. The traffic cop from the corner at Fourteenth Street was running toward them. Ram Singh was standing beside Wentworth, gun in hand, keeping the crowd at its distance.

Wentworth said urgently: "Come Quickly, Ram Singh. We must not be held here. We have work to do!"

He led the Sikh away from the crowd, away from the

He leaped squarely into the torturers' guns.

approaching policeman. The bluecoat shouted: "Hey, you! Stop! Stop, or I'll shoot!"

Wentworth and Ram Singh paid no attention to the policeman's shout. They leaped into Wentworth's cab and the Spider thrust his gun against the back of the driver's head. "Drive quickly. Get away from here!"

The cold muzzle of the gun was sufficient urging for the cabby. He threw the car into gear and sped away, down Broadway. Ram Singh had picked up Wentworth's briefcase and cane as they ran, and he put them on the seat.

Behind them another cab was swiftly giving chase, with the patrolman on the running board. Ram Singh grinned, knocked out the glass of the rear window with the butt of his revolver, then aimed a shot at the front wheel of the pursuing taxi. The tire exploded with a loud bang, and the cab swerved, almost mounted the sidewalk before the driver fought it back into control. By that time Wentworth's cab had gained almost a full block.

At the next corner Wentworth made his driver turn right, then left, then right again. At Seventh Avenue and Tenth Street they got out and ordered the driver to keep going down the one-way street. They hailed another cab, got into it, and drove for ten blocks, then changed cabs once more. By the time they had got down to Sutter Street they had thrown off all pursuit.

WENTWORTH LAUGHED harshly. "We're doing almost as well as the Dictator's gangsters, Ram Singh." He looked at the Sikh's unfamiliar, clean-shaven face, and smiled.

"You must be very deeply devoted to me, Ram Singh, to have cut off your beard for my sake."

Ram Singh lowered his eyes. "I could not help it, *sahib*. The *memsahib* Nita would have given me no peace if I had stopped following you. And you would surely have noticed me with the beard."

"And what of Miss Van Sloan?"

Ram Singh put out a hand impressively: "I beg you, *sahib*, do not be angry with me. I disobeyed you only because—"

"Yes, yes, I know," Wentworth told him. "Because you love me so." He sighed. "Maybe if you loved me less you would obey me more. I am afraid that Nita is in danger. This Dictator knows almost everything that there is to be known. He seems to have spies everywhere. He will know, of course, my connection with Nita. And with only Jackson to defend her—"

Ram Singh broke in awkwardly: "*Sahib*, there is something more I must tell you. Jackson—he, too, is not with Nita. He, too, follows you."

Wentworth's eyes suddenly flared with anger. "What! You mean to say that you have left Nita without protection?"

Ram Singh spread out both hands in a gesture of hopelessness. "What could we do, Master? She ordered it. She insisted on it. Nothing would please her but that we keep you under observation day and night."

"Ram Singh," Wentworth said solemnly, "if anything happens to Nita, I shall hold you personally responsible. And I give you warning, that the next time an order of mine is disobeyed, it will be the last order I shall ever give you!"

The faithful Sikh looked so crestfallen that Wentworth suddenly put a hand on his knee. "All right, Ram Singh, I forgive you this time. We will call Nita at the first opportunity and make sure she is safe. Where is Jackson?"

"He followed you into Casey Grogan's Dance Hall, *sahib*. He remained there. I do not know where he is."

Wentworth was worried. He hoped that Jackson would do nothing indiscreet in Grogan's place. Now he thrust all that from him. The cab was approaching the Tombs.

He had to see Evelyn Appleton, and he had to do it quickly. Also, he must find some way to discover further information about the Dictator's plans for the operation at Grand Central Station which Wishard had mentioned. *Tonight at midnight,* Wishard had said. He glanced at his watch. It was almost seven-thirty. He was due back at Casey Grogan's in an hour. But that would have to wait. This other thing that Wishard had mentioned—he must be free to work on it tonight, not hampered by a job in a dance hall.

They got out of the cab two blocks from the Tombs, and walked down. Wentworth was taking a chance—a double chance—in coming here now. First, the appeal of Evelyn Appleton might be a trap in itself; second, there would no doubt be an alarm out for a person of his description as being the one who had fled from the scene of Wishard's murder at Fourteenth Street. But the Spider was taking big chances tonight.

He left Ram Singh at the corner, and approached the Tombs alone. His eyes narrowed as he scanned the street. There seemed to be a good deal of activity on Center Street tonight. Four or five cars were parked at intervals along the curb. He passed three groups of men who seemed to be conversing idly among themselves, but who bore a furtive and tense expression. They looked him over carefully as he passed them.

There were no policemen in sight. Wentworth wondered if Argyle Dunning had removed the police from this section as he had done from the neighborhood of the Pandora Theatre earlier in the evening. There could be only one explanation for this unusual gathering around the gloomy old prison at this hour of the night—the Dictator had set his trap for the Spider.

Wentworth changed his plans instantly to suit the conditions. He passed by the entrance of the Tombs, and did not turn in. Glancing in casually, he noted that the door was open so that he could see into the small waiting room. He got a glimpse of a young woman and of three or four men inside. That young woman would be Evelyn Appleton, he had no doubt. The quick glance he got at her face showed him that she seemed to be under a great strain of some sort.

THE DOOR of the prison had been opened to permit another woman to leave. This other woman was older than Evelyn Appleton, dark and svelte. Wentworth's heart skipped a beat. He recognized her. Probing back into the recesses of his memory, he fished that older woman's name out of a dim and murky past. She would be Olga Laminoff.

He remembered her well. Olga Laminoff, the international adventuress. She and a certain Count Calypsa had been arrested and tried in France, many years ago, as the guiding geniuses of a huge mass murder plot. Calypsa and the Laminoff woman had been sentenced to Devil's Island for life; but they had escaped when the prison ship which was bearing them to their banishment was wrecked off the Azores. They had not been heard from for many years, and the police had marked them down as dead, thinking they had perished in that wreck. At times rumors penetrated the underworld that Count Calypsa was operating now here, now there. And crimes of fiendish ingenuity in widely-scattered places over the globe had borne all the earmarks of the Count's cunning hand.

Now this woman was coming out of the Tombs!

By no sign did Wentworth betray the fact that he recognized her, or even noticed her. He continued to walk slowly past the prison. Olga Laminoff came out and started in the opposite direction. Wentworth's pulse was racing. He wanted to follow that woman.

Her presence here indicated that she was connected in some way with the campaign of the Dictator. If that were the case, then the Dictator must be Count Calypsa.

That would be reason enough for the Dictator's hood. Count Calypsa's face appeared on the wanted list of every police department in the world. If he was seen he would be immediately apprehended.

But it was impossible that the Dictator should forever remain behind his hood. There must be times when he came out into the open. There must be times when he mingled as an ordinary man with other men and women. He must have some other personality—some other identity under which he posed. Could he be any one of the men whose names had so far been connected with this case—men who occupied a high position in the city's life?

Wentworth recalled that Hugh Varner had come to New York not so many years ago from Australia. He had come with excellent recommendations, had brought with him a certificate indicating that he had been a barrister in New South Wales. He had taken the necessary examination, and had been admitted to the New York Bar, then had simply developed such powerful financial connections that he had become attorney to the largest banking syndicate in the East. Could it be that Hugh Varner was Count Calypsa?

In these days of facial surgery, the Count might have done away with the true Hugh Varner in Australia, might have had his features changed, and come here posing as the attorney. But a man as clever as the Count would not have left such an easy trail to himself by giving his telephone number to Martin Kreamer.

This woman, Olga Laminoff, might give him the answer. But he dared not turn around and follow her now. There were too many men here in the street, and they were very obviously watching him. They would know that the Spider would come to meet Evelyn Appleton. They would know that he would devise some means of entering the Tombs. And they would know that he would come in disguise. So they suspected every man who approached the Tombs. If he were to turn to follow Olga Lami-noff now, it would be as if he shouted at the top of his lungs to these men: "I am the Spider!"

He must, perforce, let her go. But there was just the chance that Ram Singh would recognize her. Ram Singh was around the corner which she must pass as she walked north. Ram Singh had been with Wentworth in those days when they had known Calypsa and the Laminoff woman. Would Ram Singh recognize her?

He let the Laminoff woman walk her way, and continued past the entrance of the Tombs, crossed the street and walked down along the broad facade of the Criminal Courts Building, which was connected with the Tombs by the grim, notorious old Bridge of Sighs over which thousands of prisoners had marched after being convicted.

Wentworth glanced behind once, and saw Olga Laminoff get into a car at the far corner. He also saw that three of the watching men had detached themselves from one of the groups, and were coming down after him. Even if they did not suspect him as yet of being the Spider, they were doing their job thoroughly; they no doubt were investigating everyone who appeared on that street at this time. The Spider would have to work fast if he were to meet Evelyn Appleton in the Tombs under the very eyes of these men.

NOT DARING to hasten his stride, he turned the corner and went swiftly to the side entrance of the Criminal Courts Building. This entrance, he knew, would be open all night to permit the entrance and the egress of the porters and the cleaning women. For a moment he was out of sight of the three men who had started after him, and he slipped quickly in through this entrance, made his way upstairs. He was unobserved as he made his way swiftly through the deserted corridors into the empty detention room, and out to the hall that led into the Bridge of Sighs.

He crossed the Bridge of Sighs, looking down from the barred windows into the street below. He saw the waiting cars, and the waiting gunmen, then passed swiftly to the other end of the bridge, where there was a gate barring further progress into the Tombs. A uniformed attendant stood on the other side of the gate, and rose suspiciously as Wentworth approached.

The attendant exclaimed: "Say, what are you doing here—"

Wentworth gave him no further chance to finish. He wasted no time on the man. His cane came up, and the end of it jabbed viciously, unexpectedly through the bars into the pit of the man's stomach. The attendant uttered a low, choked cry, and doubled up in agony, clutching at his stomach.

Wentworth said: "I'm sorry, friend, but this is absolutely necessary." He reversed the cane, stuck it through the bars, and brought it down lightly on the side of the man's head behind the left ear. The man groaned, crumpled on the floor. Wentworth had struck him just hard enough to render him unconscious.

Now the Spider reached in through the bar, and with the edge of his cane he pushed the lever which released the lock on the gate. He pushed the gate open and stepped through. He was in the Tombs!

No one had heard the sound of the attendant's challenge, or of the blow which Wentworth had struck him. Now Wentworth worked swiftly, slipping off his own coat and putting on the uniform jacket of the attendant. He took the attendant's cap, left his briefcase and cane lying beside the man's body, and hurried through the corridor to the stairs leading down into the reception room. He walked in boldly, and threw a quick glance around the room.

Evelyn Appleton was backed against the wall, and two of the three men who were in the room with her were facing her savagely. One of them was saying: "When this here Spider comes, you'll act natural, understand? You give him any kind of warning, and we'll burn you down first!"

All three of the men had guns in their fists. The outer door was now closed, and a man in a keeper's uniform was standing beside it. The keeper was watching the proceedings dispassionately. The thought flashed across Wentworth's mind that this Dictator must indeed be powerful—for he apparently had the personnel of the prison under his control. The keepers were permitting his gunmen to set their traps within the very walls of the Tombs.

Evelyn Appleton shrank from the menacing guns of the gunmen. She was about to speak, when one of them turned and noticed Wentworth. "What do you want?" he growled. "Didn't the Warden get orders to keep everybody out of this reception room while we were here?"

"I'm sorry," Wentworth said, "but the Warden just got a phone call from your boss. He wants to talk to Miss Appleton on the wire. He says you men better stay down here in case something breaks. I'll take her up."

There was no suspicion in the gunman's voice as he said: "All right. Take her upstairs and bring her right down again. The Spider is liable to be here any minute."

Evelyn Appleton was glad of any excuse to get away from those men. She hurried to Wentworth's side, and just then the keeper at the door said: "Say, how come I don't know you? I've never seen you around here before."

"I'm the relief man," Wentworth began. "I just came on tonight—"

The keeper shook his head. "That can't be. I checked in everybody on the job when they came to work tonight. You weren't here."

The gunmen in the room suddenly tensed. One of them stepped forward, eyes narrowed, raising his gun. He sneered: "So, you're—"

He never finished. Wentworth had left the four top buttons of his tunic open, and now his hands darted in and out from his shoulder holsters, while at the same time he leaped sideways, thrusting Evelyn Appleton out of the way. The gunman's revolver blasted, but Wentworth was not there.

The Spider's guns began to bark in quick staccato succession as he sprayed the room with lead. For the space of a minute the small chamber was filled with the acrid smell of cordite, and with the screams of men who were shot. Wentworth was firing from the floor now, and each shot was placed with deadly accuracy.

One of the gunmen, who had started to rush toward him, died with a bullet between the eyes, and his body fell across Wentworth. Wentworth fired from behind the dead man's body, hit the last of the gunmen, just as the uniformed keeper at the door managed to get his gun out from its holster.

The keeper leveled the weapon at Wentworth, and the Spider's last shot caught him in the shoulder, sending him spinning around. The man dropped the gun, shrieked with pain. He crawled along the floor, trying to pick up his gun in his left hand, but Wentworth stepped in and struck him across the temple with the butt of his automatic. The man dropped like a log.

Swiftly Wentworth stooped beside the dead men, drew the platinum cigarette lighter from his pocket, and implanted the seal of the Spider upon the foreheads of the dead men. He laughed harshly. "A little momento for the Dictator—from the Spider!"

HE AROSE and seized Evelyn Appleton by the arm. She was pale, horrified at the sight of the sudden slaughter. But he gave her no breathing space.

"Come on, Miss Appleton," he urged her crisply. "We've got to get out of here!"

She followed him out of the reception room, asking: "W-who are you? W-what do you want?"

He didn't answer, but rushed her up the steps. In the rear of the building they could hear a commotion, the sound of men's shouting voices and running feet. Prisoners in the tiers above began banging on their cell doors, shouting and screaming. Wentworth dashed upstairs, grimly regardless of all of it.

At the Bridge of Sighs gate, the attendant was still lying unconscious. Wentworth stripped off his uniform tunic, put on his coat once more, and snatched up his briefcase and cane. Then, as he inserted new clips in his automatics, he pushed Evelyn

Appleton ahead of him across the bridge and down the stairs of the Criminal Courts Building.

In a moment they were outside in the street. The three men who had followed Wentworth down the street were standing outside, apparently wondering how he had disappeared. One of their cars had also pulled up to the curb, apparently following them for support. There was only one man in the car, at the wheel.

When the three saw Wentworth, they uttered a shout, and guns leaped into their hands. Wentworth met their fire with fire. The split instant of time by which he was faster than they cost those men their lives. His slugs sent them reeling backward, dead almost before they could fire a shot. Each of Wentworth's bullets were catapulted out of his automatics with the deadly accuracy of expert marksmanship, aimed for a vital spot. Two died with bullets between their eyes, the third with a slug right through his heart.

The driver of the sedan had drawn a gun, and he was leaning out of the door to take a shot at Wentworth. Evelyn Appleton screamed a warning, but Wentworth did not need it. His right hand gun moved in a short arc, and a single slug crashed straight into the side of the driver's head. The man slumped over the open window of the door, half in and half out of the car.

Feet were pounding on the sidewalk around the corner, and men were shouting within the Criminal Courts Building and the Tombs Building. Wentworth wasted no time. He wrenched open the door of the sedan, pushed the dead driver out onto the sidewalk, and leaped in behind the wheel. Evelyn Appleton needed no instruction. She jumped in beside him and slammed the door just as Wentworth threw the car into gear and stepped down on the gas.

He raced across town, and swung north on Broadway. Behind him the mad excitement of the chase died away. He drove in silence, fiercely, grimly, until he had lost every vestige of the pursuit.

Evelyn Appleton sat beside him, restless, wide-eyed, marveling at the skill and dexterity of his sure driving. He cut west, then swung north on Eleventh Avenue. All was quiet here. He glimpsed a police radio car cutting in from Twenty-third Street, and automatically slowed up so as not to attract their suspicion. They passed the police car in safety, and then Evelyn Appleton spoke.

"You—you are the Spider?" she asked in a hushed voice.

"I am," he told her. "You wanted to see me?"

She nodded. "I did. But I was hoping against hope that you wouldn't come. Those men were spread out all around the Tombs, and they were waiting for you in the reception room. I never dared to hope that you could escape if you once entered the Tombs. But—you did it. You accomplished the impossible. I—I'm glad I sent for you."

Wentworth glanced sideways at her. She was blonde, pretty, young. Her fresh young eyes looked at him with trusting innocence. "I—I feel safe in your hands, now, Spider. I—I almost feel as if everything will be all right. If only Frank were out of jail!"

"We'll get him out, never fear, Miss Appleton," Wentworth said. "You stated to the newspaper reporters that you had important information for me. What is it? Speak quickly. There is much to be done tonight. Your sweetheart is not the only one in danger. The whole city is under the shadow of this Dictator."

"Yes, yes," she exclaimed eagerly. "There's a woman—her name is Olga Laminoff. She is the one who originally gave me the idea to appeal to you. She came and said she had been a friend of father's. She suggested that I get in touch with you. And it was she who suggested that I wait for you at the Tombs.

"But I learned that she was lying. She was never a friend of father's. From the conversation of those men in the Tombs I gathered that she is closely linked in some way with the Dictator. And they were talking carelessly near me earlier in the day. They were talking about some great coup that the Dictator expects to pull off tonight at midnight. It's going to be at Grand Central Station. I heard that all police are to be withdrawn from the neighborhood of Grand Central. And there's going to be a monster holdup there."

Wentworth nodded. "I already know that. But are you sure that they didn't talk about this deliberately so that you would tell me about it?"

Evelyn Appleton gasped. "I never thought of that. I thought I was being so clever in overhearing snatches of their conversation. But now that you mention it, it occurs to me that they talked unnecessarily loudly." Suddenly she put a trembling hand on his arm. "Spider! Suppose it's another trap for you? Suppose they deliberately planned it, in case this trap didn't succeed?"

Wentworth laughed harshly. "If it's a trap at midnight, we'll see if we can't spring it the way we sprung the one at the Tombs."

He swung east, drove for two blocks and halted the car in the middle of the next block near a small cigar store where there was a telephone.

"What are you going to do?" Evelyn asked.

"I'm going to get in touch with Commissioner Kirkpatrick. If Argyle Dunning has ordered the police away from Grand Central at midnight, we will have a little surprise for the Dictator. I'll get Kirkpatrick to place other police there!"

He left Evelyn Appleton sitting in the car, and hurried into the telephone booth.

CHAPTER 8
RECEPTION AT GROGAN'S

WENTWORTH DROPPED his nickel in the box and dialed police headquarters. In a moment he was talking to the operator.

"I wish to speak to Commissioner Kirkpatrick at once," he said crisply.

There was a short laugh at the other end. "Commissioner Kirkpatrick? He ain't commissioner anymore. Inspector Strong has been appointed commissioner by the Mayor. Who wants to talk to him?"

A cold chill went through Wentworth's frame. If Kirkpatrick had been ousted from headquarters, he must find him. But even if he found him, what good would it do? Without the official status of commissioner, Kirkpatrick could do nothing.

"Where is Mr. Kirkpatrick?"

"Didn't you hear it on the radio? Kirkpatrick went nuts suddenly. He's been taken in a straitjacket to The New York Hospital for the Insane, on Seventy-second Street. You'll find him there, if you want him. Ha, ha!" There was a sharp click as the operator at the other end broke the connection.

Wentworth gasped. The Dictator was moving fast now, cleverly, ruthlessly, eliminating all obstacles swiftly. With Kirkpatrick insane, there could be no question as to whether Argyle Dunning had the authority to appoint another commissioner. And Dunning had apparently done so at once.

With Inspector Strong at the head of the Police Department, and granting that Argyle Dunning acted under instructions from the hooded Dictator, there was nothing to stand in the way of the Dictator's plans. By morning he would have supreme authority in the City of New York. Wentworth didn't know yet whether Ram Singh had stayed at the corner, or had followed Olga Laminoff. In either event, Ram Singh would no doubt come looking for him in Casey Grogan's. He had to go back there to meet Ram Singh and Jackson. His original intention to work alone was gone by the board. Jackson had thrust his head into danger. So had Ram Singh. They would do that whether they were with him or not. And now he needed them, with Kirkpatrick out of the Police Department.

He returned to the car and slid in under the wheel, beside Evelyn Appleton. As they drove uptown, she asked him nervously: "Is something wrong? You're so silent. Did you get bad news?"

"Very bad news," be told her. "I'm afraid this fight is going to be tougher than we've expected." He gave her quick instructions. "I'm driving up to Casey Grogan's Dance Hall. I want you to go inside alone and ask for Krauss, the manager. Ask him for a job as a hostess. You're pretty, and young, and he'll probably give it to you. I want to keep you out of harm's way for the next three or four hours, and I think you will be as safe there as anywhere. No one will think of looking for Evelyn Appleton among the hostesses in a cheap dance hall."

Her eyes were shining eagerly. "I'll do whatever you say, Spider. I'm leaving my own fate and the fate of Frank in your hands. I—I trust you, Spider!"

"Thank you," he said softly. "I hope your trust is not misplaced."

AT FIFTY-FOURTH STREET he parked the stolen car two blocks west of Casey Grogan's Dance Hall, and sent Evelyn Appleton ahead to ask for the job. He remained in the car, and using the rear-vision mirror, he altered his features once more to become Jake Smith. His automatics were empty, and he had no more clips for them. He shrugged. He would have to go against the Dictator without guns then.

His disguise completed, he picked up the briefcase, but left the cane in the car.

He walked swiftly across Fifty-fourth Street, keeping a sharp eye out for Ram Singh, in case the Sikh should be looking for him here.

Ram Singh was there. He had been waiting in a doorway directly opposite the dance hall, from whence he could see all who approached. Wentworth paused to speak quickly:

"Ram Singh! There is much to do. I need your help."

The Sikh's face broke into a glad smile. "I am happy, *sahib*, that I can serve you. What is there to do?"

"Kirkpatrick is in The New York Hospital for the Insane, on Seventy-second Street. I am sure that he is being held there by a subterfuge, to permit the Dictator to appoint his own police commissioner. We must get Kirkpatrick out of there. I want you to go to Seventy-second Street now, and study the lay of the land. Find out what sort of hospital Kirkpatrick is in, and devise the best means for us to gain admittance to him. Arrange for a car so that we can make a getaway if we succeed in getting him out. I will meet you there within the hour. Hurry."

Ram Singh raised a hand to his forehead, salaamed. "I go, master."

He turned and went swiftly away.

Wentworth entered the dance hall, carrying the briefcase. A group of a dozen or more people stood at the entrance to the narrow corridor leading to the barroom. Krauss, the manager, faced them.

"It's nothing at all, ladies and gentlemen, nothing to worry about. Just a little argument going on in there, but nobody can go in." The group was boisterous, but did not resent being kept out of the barroom.

Wentworth frowned. He must find out what was going on in there. He swung away from the group, to the corner of the dance hall.

The Spider stepped quickly into the smoking room and glanced around to make sure that he was alone. Then he took the cape and hat out of the briefcase and slipped them on. In another moment he had inserted those long, protruding fang-like teeth which made the Spider recognizable wherever he went. Then, very carefully, he opened the door leading into the barroom.

His eyes grew bleak and hard at the sight of the tableau which greeted him.

In the center of the room stood the hooded man whom Wentworth had seen on the hearse. Beside him was the woman, Olga Laminoff. Both held guns. Over at the other end of the room, near the bar, Jackson was backed up against the wall, and two stocky, vicious men were beating him methodically. Wentworth could see the flash of brass knuckles on their fists as they struck, cutting Jackson's cheeks to ribbons.

The hooded man was saying coldly: "You had better talk, Jackson. We know who you are. You are Wentworth's chauffeur. Wentworth's girl, Nita Van Sloan, is in our hands. We want you to tell us where to get in touch with the Spider. Talk quickly. Where can we find him? You didn't come here by accident. Who sent you?"

THE SPIDER was unarmed but he didn't hesitate. Harsh, discordant, terrifying laughter broke from his lips. He leaped to his feet and vaulted onto the bar.

The hooded man and the woman Olga turned startled glances in his direction. The thugs stopped with their fists poised in midair.

Olga Laminoff gasped: "It's the Spider!"

113

The little revolver which she brandished swung around and *spatted* viciously, while the hooded man also shifted to fire.

But the Spider had already launched himself headfirst in a reckless leap directly at those two. So startled and astounded were they that they had shot before aiming. Their slugs went wild, and the Spider's solid weight of bone and muscle catapulted into them irresistibly, hurling them to the floor in a twisting, struggling heap.

Olga Laminoff screamed shrilly, and her voice rose above the blaring notes of the dance orchestra in the next room. The two thugs swung around from Jackson, and their hands sped to their shoulder holsters. Wentworth whirled over onto his knees, and his hand swept across the floor, snatched up the small gun that Olga Laminoff had dropped.

His eyes were cold, hard, unemotional as he fired twice at the two thugs. It was a small-caliber revolver, and the shots had to be placed accurately to kill. Wentworth placed both of them dead center through the forehead. The two thugs died on their feet.

Jackson shouted: "Yeah, bo!" and bent and snatched up one of the guns dropped by the thugs. Wentworth swung around in time to see the hooded man racing through the open door of Krauss' office at the other side of the barroom. He raised his gun to fire, but abruptly his arm was clutched by the almost hysterical Olga Laminoff, who sank her teeth into his hand. In that instant he heard the loud explosion of the gun that Jackson had seized.

Jackson cursed. "Missed him!" the chauffeur exclaimed. The door of Krauss' office slammed, and the hooded man disappeared. Wentworth freed his hand from between Olga's teeth, prying her jaws apart, then thrust her away from him savagely and leaped toward the door. The hooded man had locked it from the inside.

Jackson said: "Stand back, sir," and launched himself straight at the door. The wood splintered and gave under the smashing heave of his body, and Jackson went through. Wentworth leaped in over him, and stopped, eyes narrowed.

The room was empty. An open window giving on to a fire escape told its own story. Wentworth leaped through it, climbed out on the fire escape. He was just in time to see the dark shadowy figure of the hooded man turning the corner of the alley into Fifty-fourth Street.

Wentworth turned back into the room dejectedly. Through the open door he saw the barroom filling with excited people from the dance floor. Krauss was in the lead, a gun in his hand. Jackson had already picked himself up, and Wentworth snapped: "Out this way, Jackson."

They leaped out to the fire escape and raced down the emergency ladder along the way that the hooded man had taken. Behind them, shouts came from the milling crowd on the dance floor, and from behind the splintered door Krauss sprang, gun in hand. But Wentworth and Jackson were in the clear. Krauss, standing on the fire escape, fired down at them. His shot ricocheted from the iron staircase and from the concrete walk below.

Men were yelling: "It's the Spider! The Spider was here!"

Wentworth raised his pistol, fired up twice at Krauss, and the little man toppled backward through the window.

Then the Spider led Jackson quickly out of the alley into

Fifty-fourth Street. A police car had just turned the corner from Broadway, and it came to a stop in front of the dance hall. The two policemen leaped out and raced inside. Wentworth nudged Jackson. "Let's go!"

They raced out of the alley and leaped into the police radio car. Wentworth threw in the clutch and raced the car away from there.

"It's very nice of the police, sir," Jackson said, smiling, "to provide us with a means of escape."

HE WAS daubing at his cut cheeks and lips with a bloody handkerchief. "Those boys almost had me down with their brass knuckles. You came in the nick of time."

"The Dictator got away," Wentworth said bitterly. "He seems to beat us at every turn."

"At least," Jackson said cheerfully, "we're catching up with him. That was awful close back there."

They left the police squad car at Fifty-eighth Street and Ninth Avenue.

"Where to now, sir?" Jackson asked.

Wentworth led him at a swift walk across Fifty-ninth Street. He had taken off his Spider cape and hat, and had rolled it into a small bundle beneath his coat.

"I don't know where to go first," Wentworth said bitterly. "I heard the Dictator tell you that they had Nita. God help us, I don't know where to look for her first. I have no idea where she may be—"

"I'll tell you, sir. I heard that hooded man and the Laminoff woman talking. They said something about having taken her

116

to the printing plant. It seems they're running a printing plant somewhere in the city, where they're turning out a flood of tens and twenties. They expect to overrun the country with them, using New York as their headquarters. Now that they are gaining control of the city, they figure they can use New York as their base of operations."

"A printing plant? You don't know where it is, do you?"

"No, sir. The woman told the hooded man that she had just come from there. She said she thought she was followed, but she couldn't be sure."

Wentworth's eyes brightened. "Ram Singh!" he exclaimed. "Of course! Ram Singh was waiting for me outside there. He must have followed Olga Laminoff from the Tombs. Then he must know where she went before she came to Grogan's Dance Hall. Let's go, Jackson!"

They hailed a taxicab, and Wentworth gave the address of The New York Hospital for the Insane. The driver looked queerly at Jackson's cut-up face, but said nothing.

They got out of the cab at Seventieth Street, and Wentworth gave the driver a ten-dollar bill.

"That's to help you to forget you saw us," Wentworth told the man. "In case you should forget about the ten-dollar bill, and feel like talking to anybody, I'll learn about it. I've got your name and address from the card in the taxicab. I'll be able to find you, and it will be too bad for you. Understand?"

The driver grinned. "Don't worry, mister. I ain't looking for trouble. I never even saw you before."

He drove away, and Wentworth and Jackson walked swiftly

toward The New York Hospital for the Insane. Wentworth glanced at his watch. There was little time left to accomplish what he had in mind. For the time being he must leave Nita in the hands of the Dictator. His objective now was to get Kirkpatrick out of the hospital, and to organize some sort of resistance to the Dictator's plans for the coup at Grand Central Station at midnight.

CHAPTER 9
PRINTERS... AND MANIACS

O N THE edge of the East River, almost under the shadow of the Queensboro Bridge, there stands an old, dilapidated factory building. The building is only three stories high, and across its face, in the old, curlicue characters of a past generation there appears the following name:

HAMLIN'S PRINTING HOUSE
ESTABLISHED 1892

Hamlin's Printing House was a firm which had flourished in the days of the bustle and the one-horse shay. Long ago the building had been abandoned. The building seemed to be deserted. But within its walls was a surprising activity. Though the windows were boarded up, and no sound or light came from within, machines hummed here industriously.

Huge modern printing presses turned out United States Treasury certificates at appalling speed. Forty men worked in this building, and stacks of the currency were rolled on small hand-trucks down into the basement, where they were loaded onto tow boats that took them on the first leg of their journey to be distributed throughout the country. In the basement, the huge wheel of a turbine engine had been disconnected from the adjacent machinery.

Half a dozen men worked at this wheel. They had erected a smaller wheel, a sort of controlling mechanism, by which they could turn the larger wheel. They were oiling all the parts of the mechanism now, and testing it to see whether it was running smoothly.

In a corner of this basement, two figures lay on the floor, tightly bound. They were so placed that they could see the men working on the huge wheel, could see where the wheel dipped at its bottom into a tract of water, perhaps two feet deep. The eyes of both of these bound persons were alive with interest, if not with fear.

One of them was Nita Van Sloan. The other was little Elaine Robillard.

Though they were tied hand and foot, they had not been gagged; and little Elaine said in a hushed whisper: "Nita, those are very bad men. They were very rough when they took us away from the house. Why are men so rough?"

Nita's pitying eyes rested for a moment on the little girl. She choked back a sob. The thought of this child in the hands of these men was more than she could bear. For herself she did not care. When the Dictator's men had come for her at the penthouse apartment, she might have escaped had she been alone. She had snatched up a revolver, and would have fired. But Elaine

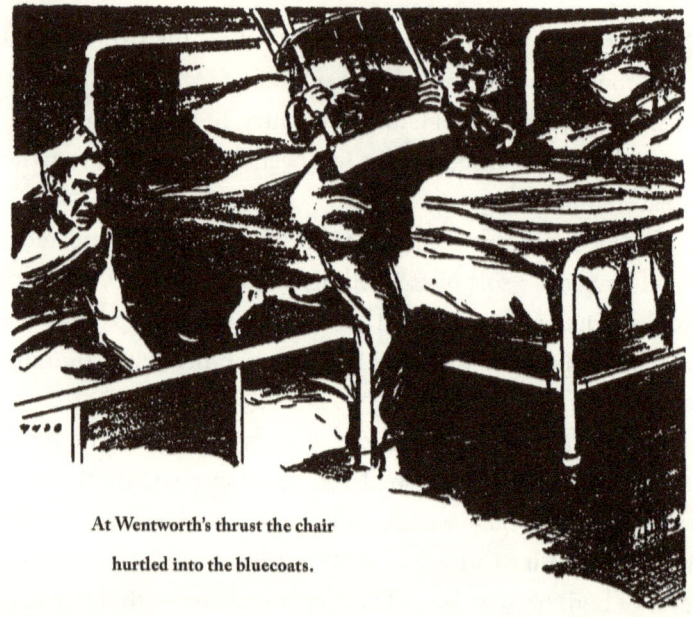

At Wentworth's thrust the chair
hurtled into the bluecoats.

Robillard had come running out of the next room, directly in the line of fire.

And they had both been seized and hustled down in the freight elevator, blindfolded and thrust into a car which had swiftly carried them to this place.

Now as Nita Van Sloan looked at the huge turbine wheel and at the men working on it, she shuddered. She felt as those old French aristocrats must have felt while they watched the guillotine being erected outside the Bastille.

She knew that this wheel was some fiendish method of torture or death which had been devised for her benefit by the Dictator. The Dictator hated Wentworth, hated everything

connected with Wentworth. And he was taking this means of venting that hatred.

To Nita, the horrid thing about all this was the utter silence with which those men were working. One might have thought that they were concentrated there upon some complicated structural problem of engineering rather than upon a task of erecting a machine of torture. No one threw a single glance in their direction; it was as if they, as persons, did not exist for those workers.

And looking down upon it all from the lintel of the doorway, which led to the staircase, was the gold-encrusted symbol of the lion crouching upon the crown, with the sword and the mitre in his forepaws. Whoever the artist was that had placed that insignia above the doorway, he was clever, malevolently ingenious. For he had imparted to that king of beasts so malignant an expression that Nita shuddered even to look at the lion.

By this time she had learned enough about the Dictator to know his aims and ambitions. And that lion sitting upon the crown summed up the desires and lust of the master of the underworld; he wanted power. He wanted to rule, to rule ruthlessly and without question. And he was bringing it about by establishing an underworld organization more powerful than any that had yet threatened the civilization of a country.

Elaine was quiet now, watching Nita, taking courage from her. And Nita's brows were furrowed in thought as she tried to imagine who this Dictator could be in the upper world.

That he was one whom everybody saw and knew, there could be no doubt; for otherwise he would never have been able to establish the widespread connections that he seemed to have.

But who could this person be? With less information than Wentworth possessed at this time, she was even more puzzled.

She knew that Argyle Dunning had demanded the resignation of Kirkpatrick; but she did not yet know that Kirkpatrick had been removed to the Hospital for the Insane. She could not bring herself to imagine that a man like Argyle Dunning would deliberately conspire to seize his own nephew for murder in order to further his interests; yet, noting the fiendish ruthlessness with which the Dictator had operated since the beginning of his campaign, she was forced to admit to herself that he might even be ready to sacrifice a close relative in order to attain his ambition.

WHILE NITA VAN SLOAN was cogitating upon these things in the basement where the wheel was being erected, the hooded man and Olga Laminoff were seated in an office on the floor directly above. Four men, including Martin Kreamer, were facing the Dictator, while Olga sat at the desk at his right. Kreamer was making a report, while the other three men standing with him shifted uncomfortably, their eyes upon the gold-encrusted figure of the lion which was engraved upon the narrow hanging draped behind the Dictator's chair.

The hooded man was sitting quietly at the desk, nothing showing of his face except two lively sparkling eyes behind the slits in the hood.

"We have succeeded in every operation, sir," Kreamer was saying, "except those involving the Spider. With the Spider we have failed all along the line. That man seems to appear out of nowhere. He got Sorenson and Masters, two of my best operators, when they were knocking off Wishard. Then he sprang the trap we laid for him at the Tombs, and spirited Evelyn Appleton out of our hands. We don't know where she is now."

The hooded man nodded. "Not only that, but he barged right into Casey Grogan's place and snatched his man Jackson right out of our hands. We were just beginning to succeed in breaking Jackson down. He would have talked, would have given us information as to the Spider's whereabouts. And just then the Spider himself appeared. He hadn't even a gun. But he moved so fast that he almost killed *me*. A half second more and I would never have escaped from that barroom alive."

Suddenly the hooded man's gloved fist slammed down on the desk viciously. "I tell you, Kreamer, we've got to get the Spider. You failed miserably so far. *See to it that you don't fail again!*"

"I—I won't fail again, sir. I think the Spider is going to walk right into our trap at Grand Central tonight. I made sure that Evelyn Appleton learned enough to tell him that we are staging an operation at Grand Central tonight. I originally planned to leave him with her for a couple of minutes so that she could tell him that, just the way you instructed me. I couldn't see the reason for it at the time you gave me the instructions, but now I understand. You just wanted to make sure there would be another trap for him in case the one at the Tombs failed."

Olga Laminoff broke in, her voice vibrant: "I wonder if the Spider isn't a super-man. Who would have thought it possible that he could snatch Evelyn Appleton right out of the Tombs, with forty of our men surrounding it—"

The Dictator laughed harshly. "We overlooked the entrance

through the Bridge of Sighs. Be sure, my dear Olga, that we will overlook nothing at the Grand Central tonight. Once the Spider enters that station, *there will be no way for him to leave alive.* Argyle Dunning has removed all police from the entire Grand Central sector for a radius of ten blocks in every direction. We will be entirely unhampered in the operation. We will secure enough cash to finance us until this newly-printed money can be distributed; and we will get the Spider, too."

"But," Olga Laminoff broke in, "why are you preparing all that complicated business downstairs for the Van Sloan woman?"

"For the same reason that I left an opening for a second trap after the Tombs. If by any wild chance the plan at Grand Central Station falls through, we will still have the Van Sloan woman here. And we shall start prying information from her at once. In China, nobody has ever been able to resist the persuasion of the water-wheel. She will talk. She will tell us where Wentworth is holed up."

The Dictator turned to the three other men. "You three are ready to leave at once?"

They nodded.

"Good. All arrangements have been made at the other end. You, Lasher, will take off at once for New Orleans. Franco, you go to Chicago. Bourdon, Montreal for you. The planes are all ready and waiting for you out on Long Island. The counterfeit bills have all been loaded on the planes, and two armed men will accompany each of you.

"See that the people at the other end put nothing over on you. They are to pay in cash—good American currency—for the bills that you deliver to them. You three are all experts, and can tell a counterfeit bill when you see it. Don't let them pay you for counterfeit money with other counterfeit money. Now, go."

The three men bowed, and left the room. The Dictator looked at Kreamer. "All arrangements are made for Grand Central Station?"

"Yes, sir. It's timed to the second, and everybody has been given his instructions. The thing should go off like clockwork."

"Very well. You may go."

Kreamer bowed, and followed the other three out of the room. The Dictator and Olga Laminoff were left alone. He rubbed his gloved hand, said in a voice that had suddenly become thick with cruelty:

"Come, my dear Olga. We shall now turn our attention to the beautiful Nita Van Sloan and that brat with her."

He arose, and Olga followed him to the door. She asked, puzzled: "Just what are you going to do to them?"

"Come, my dear Olga. You shall see. It will be far more interesting than if I merely explain it to you."

She followed him downstairs toward the cellar where the wheel was being completed....

THE NEW YORK HOSPITAL FOR THE INSANE was located on Seventy-second Street, with a view of Central Park. It was a small, four-story, immaculately white institution, from its newly sandblasted walls on the outside to its spotlessly clean detention cells on the inside.

At the rear of the ground floor was the observation ward. There were some twenty patients in this ward, of whom half were in straitjackets, while the others lay peaceably in their beds without any precautions to prevent their escape.

Two New York City patrolmen were stationed at the door of the ward, while at the other end, near the window, stood two hard-faced thugs who always kept their hands in the pockets of their coats. These were two of Kreamer's operators, Landers and Mollat. Their sharp, pinpoint eyes were fixed upon the third bed from the end, away from the window, where lay Commissioner Stanley Kirkpatrick.

Kirkpatrick was motionless on the bed. He was clad in pajamas, and the upper part of his body was firmly and cruelly encased in a straitjacket. His ankles were handcuffed to the bedpost. He lay with his eyes closed, breathing with great difficulty because of the wicked pressure exerted upon his chest by the straitjacket.

Others of the patients were talking, shouting, laughing hysterically. The din and the noise in the room were almost deafening; yet all these patients cast occasional glances of trepidation not at the two policemen, but at the two thugs at the other end of the room. Those two men had been placed there by Kreamer for the sole purpose of making sure that no efforts would be made to rescue Kirkpatrick.

Dr. Vladimir Ostrevsky, the director of the hospital, entered the ward. Ostrevsky was a short man, with a high, bald head and big ears. His eyes protruded from his head like the eyes of some predatory prehistoric animal. But his hands were long and thin, and he walked with a birdlike jumpiness that was very irritating.

The New York Hospital for the Insane had been in the founders' hands for many years; about six months before, it had been taken over by new interests. It seemed that the old board of governors had by some means been induced to resign, and give place to a new controlling circle.

This new board boasted some very influential men, among them Argyle Dunning, Hugh Varner, and Stephen Pelton. Dr. Ostrevsky had been appointed director, and he had immediately proceeded to discharge all of the old nurses, internes and doctors, and to acquire a completely new staff.

The doctor minced down the aisle between the two rows of beds, stopping occasionally beside a patient. He would look at the man, with his bald head cocked on one side, mutter something to himself, then turn away and proceed to the next patient.

The din and the noise had suddenly ceased with Dr. Ostrevsky's entrance. The poor, insane patients glanced with terror at those long thin surgeon's hands of his. Apparently they recalled an unpleasant experience which they had undergone at those hands. Had they been questioned, they would have suddenly become silent on the subject. But many of them remembered with horror the small operating room on the top floor of the hospital where they had been taken and tied down to an operating table. Dr. Ostrevsky had manipulated with gleaming knives and saws upon their quivering, conscious bodies.

For the good doctor was an experimentalist. And he took this opportunity of testing many of his theories. These poor devils would have obeyed any command from Dr. Ostrevsky rather than be subjected to that experience again.

Now, the birdlike doctor approached the bed of Commissioner Kirkpatrick.

As though he sensed the malignant presence of Ostrevsky, Kirkpatrick opened his eyes. His lips tightened, and he glared up at the little man.

"Damn you!" he shouted hoarsely. "Let me out of here. Take this damned straitjacket off!"

Ostrevsky looked down at him with mock sympathy, and clucked gently. "Tut, tut, Mr. Kirkpatrick. You must realize that you are here for your own good. I trust that within a reasonable time I shall be able to cure you of this dreadful malady that afflicts you—"

"Dreadful malady, nothing, you old humbug!" Kirkpatrick shouted. "You know very well I'm not insane—"

Ostrevsky was shaking his head in resignation. "So many of our poor patients insist that they are not crazy. Perhaps you even think that we are the crazy ones—no?"

"Ostrevsky," Kirkpatrick said solemnly, "I promise you that if I ever get out of this straitjacket, I'll throttle you with my own hands."

"That is a threat which I shall remember, Mr. Kirkpatrick. Perhaps—" he bent low and almost whispered the next words— *"you will never come out of that straitjacket!"*

Kirkpatrick's eyes widened at the look of stark evil in the doctor's face.

Ostrevsky went on: "Poor Mr. Harlan Foote was brought here, in a condition like yours. It was so regretful. I had to operate on him, and he died under the knife!"

Kirkpatrick gasped. "You're going to—operate—on me?"

Ostrevsky nodded. "Upon diagnosing your case, Mr. Kirkpatrick, I find that it will be *most* desirable to operate upon you at once. We are going to move you upstairs. The interne is bringing in the wheelchair now. Prepare yourself, my dear patient, for a very—er—unpleasant ordeal. I do not believe in administering anesthetics, so you will be entirely conscious during the operation. You will have an opportunity to see how very skillfully I manipulate a scalpel."

Kirkpatrick heaved tremendously, but could not raise himself from the bed. He yanked violently with his feet against the handcuffs that bound his ankles to the bed, but succeeded only in bruising himself. Several of the other patients who had been watching the scene, but were unable to hear the latter part of the conversation, began to shout and scream once more. They knew what was coming, because they had seen Ostrevsky talk to others.

The noise of their insane shoutings became dreadful, and Ostrevsky swung around, letting his eyes pass from one to the other of the patients; and as he looked at them in turn, each became suddenly silent. They looked away from him, as if fearful that he would decide to operate upon them.

Ostrevsky glanced at the big electric clock over the door. He frowned in impatience.

"What is keeping the interne with the chair, I wonder?" he asked softly. He shrugged. "But do not grow impatient, my dear Mr. Kirkpatrick!"

DR. OSTREVSKY did not know that the interne whom he

130

was expecting was at that very moment standing with his back to the wall in the outside corridor, with his hands raised above his head. There was a man on either side of him.

The chair stood near by.

The interne didn't know them, but he was quaking at sight of the grim resolve in their eyes. The snub-nosed automatic which Jackson held at his side enforced the commands of the interne's chief captor. While Jackson had him covered, Wentworth motioned to him peremptorily: "Turn around!"

The man turned obediently, and Wentworth twisted his hands behind his back, and reached around to remove the man's belt with which to bind them. At that moment the interne chose to open his mouth to shriek a warning.

Wentworth sensed what he was going to do, and his hand bunched into a hard fist, came up in a vicious blow to the side of the man's jaw. The interne groaned, the shout died in his throat, and he slumped unconscious to the floor.

Jackson grunted: "That's much quicker, sir. He won't bother us for awhile."

Wentworth nodded. From his pocket he took a gun which he had received from Ram Singh when he and Jackson had met the Sikh outside the hospital. Ram Singh was waiting outside.

Wentworth held the gun in his right hand, and wheeled the empty wheelchair toward the observation ward. He said to Jackson: "Wait out here, and be ready to cover my retreat when I come out."

"Yes, sir," Jackson said, saluting stiffly. He grinned. "Give 'em hell, sir!"

Wentworth wheeled the chair down the corridor, and into the observation room, past the two patrolmen at the door. His quick glance surveyed the room, showed him the two thugs near the window, and Ostrevsky leaning over Kirkpatrick's bed.

The policemen glanced at him suspiciously, seeing his street clothes, but were reassured as they saw the wheelchair. The two thugs were paying no attention to him, but were watching with gloating eyes the reaction of Kirkpatrick to the vile things Ostrevsky was promising to do to him.

Wentworth reached the bed before Dr. Ostrevsky knew that he was there. The doctor raised his head, saw the wheelchair out of the side of his eyes, and swung around, saying grumpily: "You're late—"

His mouth jerked open, hung slack, as he saw that the regular interne had not brought in the chair. "W-who are you—"

Wentworth gave him no chance to finish. He moved close to the doctor, stuck the gun in his side. "If you don't want your liver blasted out of you, doc, do as I say. Pick up Kirkpatrick, quickly, and put him in that wheelchair."

The two thugs suddenly became aware that trouble was brewing, and they reached for their guns, just as the patrolmen at the door did likewise. Wentworth raised his voice coldly. "If any one of you so much as moves, Ostrevsky dies!"

The thugs hesitated, as did the patrolmen. Ostrevsky said, smirking, "I'm sorry, but Kirkpatrick cannot be moved. He is handcuffed to the bed, as you see, and I have not the key."

Wentworth said softly: "I see!"

He seized Ostrevsky's left arm, twisted it hard behind his

back, and Ostrevsky gasped from the sudden pain. One of the thugs pulled a gun from his pocket, but Wentworth swung the doctor around in such fashion that he was directly in the line of fire. The thug hesitated. In that instant, Wentworth acted. He swung his automatic away from Ostrevsky's side, placed it close to one of the handcuffs on the bedpost, and fired. The steel was shattered by the heavy slug, and Wentworth immediately moved his gun, fired another shot into the second handcuff.

"Pull, Kirk!" he ordered.

Kirkpatrick yanked hard with both feet, and the handcuffs fell away from the bedpost.

Wentworth now swung around so as to face the ward, with Kirkpatrick behind him. He still held Ostrevsky powerless in front of him, by the arm-lock. "Can you walk, Kirk?" he asked over his shoulder.

"God!" the Commissioner groaned. "I can barely raise myself." The bed creaked under his weight, and the Commissioner tottered to his feet. The long period of inactivity had made him weak. But he managed to totter over to the wheelchair and slump into it.

One of the thugs now swung his gun around to fire at Kirkpatrick, and Wentworth snapped a shot, shattered the thug's shoulder. Ostrevsky shouted, and twisted away. The two policemen had come rushing forward, and Wentworth sent the doctor spinning dizzily across the room toward the cops, who sprang to save him from falling.

Wentworth leaped into the aisle, seized the wheelchair and began rushing it toward the door. The policemen raised their guns to fire at him, but Wentworth sent the wheelchair racing down the aisle directly at them, and one of them was bowled over, while the other barely leaped out of the way.

Behind Wentworth, the two thugs were firing at him, the wounded one having switched his gun to the left hand. Wentworth swung around and snapped two shots at the thugs, aiming deliberately at their hearts. He caught them both dead center, then leaped after the racing wheelchair.

The maniacs in the ward who were not confined by straitjackets were leaping about frenziedly, shouting and screaming at the top of their lungs. Several of them had seized chairs and were leaping out into the aisle to strike at Wentworth. He dodged the blows, menacing them with his revolver, barely managing to keep them at arm's length.

The policeman who had leaped out of the way of the wheelchair was crouching behind one of the beds, raising his gun to fire at Wentworth. Wentworth crouched, and just then one of the maniacs leaped in on him, raising a chair to smash it down on his head. Wentworth dropped flat to the floor, and the maniac went flying over him. The policeman fired at just that instant, and the slug from the service gun caught the maniac in the leg. The man shrieked and doubled over.

Wentworth got to his feet and sprinted for the doorway. Kirkpatrick's chair had rolled into the corridor, and now Wentworth seized it again, raced for the front entrance. He passed Jackson, who was coolly kneeling in the corridor, gun in hand and facing toward the observation ward.

"Keep going, sir," Jackson called out cheerfully. "I'll hold them."

THE MANIACS, with one of the cops in their midst, came piling out of the observation ward. Near the entrance the attendant at the desk got to his feet and came running forward. Wentworth swung the wheelchair with Kirkpatrick in it toward the attendant, and the man leaped out of the way.

At the door, Wentworth wheeled the chair out onto the sidewalk, and over to the curb where Ram Singh sat grinning in a taxicab. Ram Singh leaped out and helped Wentworth to pile the Commissioner into the cab.

The Sikh said, showing his teeth: "The cab driver did not want to lend me his cab, *sahib*. I had to persuade him with this." He tapped his sheathed knife significantly.

They had Kirkpatrick in the cab now, and Ram Singh ran around to the front and slid in under the wheel. Wentworth held the door open, and Jackson came hurtling out, leaped into the cab. Wentworth shut the door, sprang to the running board and raised his gun to menace the maniacs and the policeman, who were crowding out of the doorway of the hospital.

The policeman raised his gun to fire, but Ram Singh had already shot the cab out into the middle of the street and was racing around the corner into Fifth Avenue.

Men and women were leaning out of windows, aroused by the blood-curdling screams of the maniacs and the shots of the policemen. Ram Singh paid no attention to them, but drove steadily south on Fifth Avenue. He made no attempt to evade pursuit. The time for avoiding enemies was past. Now they must drive straight through all opposition. So had been Wentworth's orders.

In the rear of the cab, Wentworth and Jackson were busily engaged in removing the straitjacket from Commissioner Kirkpatrick. When they got it off, Kirkpatrick slumped back in the seat, and breathed deeply.

"God, what a relief! That straitjacket was almost crushing my ribs!" He looked at Wentworth. "Dick, I don't need to thank you for this. But it was reckless. You shouldn't have done it. With the city in danger, you didn't need to risk your life getting me out of there."

Wentworth grinned at him affectionately. "It wasn't only for your sake I did it, Kirk. I've got a plan in mind, and you've got to help me. If we don't put this over, the city might as well give up and choose the Dictator as its mayor."

"What's the plan?" Kirkpatrick asked swiftly. Already he had forgotten the hours of torture in the straitjacket and the ominous threat of the operating room in that weird hospital.

Wentworth spoke swiftly: "The Dictator is planning some great coup at Grand Central Station at midnight. Argyle Dunning has appointed Inspector Strong commissioner, and Strong has cleared the whole district of police. There'll be no opposition to the Dictator's men when they strike at Grand Central Station. We have to block them, Kirk. If we checkmate him at Grand Central Station, it will block his plans all along the line. He'll lose the respect of his organization. Do you understand, Kirk? We've got to stop him!"

"But how?" the ex-commissioner asked, puzzled. "I've got no

authority. He'll probably have a hundred men at Grand Central. How can we cope with that?"

"You may have no authority," Wentworth said slowly, "but you have the respect of all the honest policemen in the department. I propose, Kirk, that you set up a *sub-rosa* headquarters and enlist the aid of all the honest policemen in the city. We will have a private police headquarters in New York—until the Dictator is licked!"

Kirkpatrick whistled. "It's a swell idea, Dick—if it works!"

"It's got to work, Kirk," the Spider said through tight lips. *"It's got to work!* We've got to break the Dictator's power, and do it quickly. He kidnapped Nita and Elaine!"

CHAPTER 10
THE TORTURE WHEEL

THE CITY had an air of unquiet and restiveness now— far different than the atmosphere of quiet gaiety which Wentworth had noted as he left the office of the Five-Star Detective Agency earlier that evening.

Then, he had seen crowds of people moving through the streets, undisturbed by any thought of crime or personal danger.

Now the populace was fearful, bewildered by the strange series of events that had stunned the city.

They had heard of the strange upheavals at police headquarters, of the peculiar situation by which the nephew of the present mayor was accused of the murder of a police commissioner; they had heard of the Spider's invasion of headquarters, of Wishard's strange and unexplained murder; and they had also heard of a mysterious disturbance at the Tombs. All this, coupled with the daring robbery of the Pandora Theatre, and the strange rumors that were flooding the city of this new Dictator of the underworld, left them dazed. They saw that great areas in the city had been stripped of police protection, and they began to worry for the safety of their wives and their children. Men gathered in groups on the street corners and discussed the situation in hushed tones. Ordinarily, these citizens went about their business and their pleasure without a thought of the complicated machinery of the law which watched over their safety. Now, when that same complicated machinery was suffering a shifting of great cogs, these men abruptly realized that the city could become a scene of chaos and anarchy overnight.

And this unrest and disturbance was particularly noticeable in the streets of downtown Manhattan. Automobiles and taxicabs flagrantly passed red lights, made left turns against the rules, and violated ordinance after ordinance without reprimand from the police. The uniformed men were fumbling and worried. Ordinarily, the New York Police Force is among the best disciplined and the best-manned law-enforcing agencies in the world. But no group of men can be expected to maintain its morale and its spirit when the personnel are aware that its leadership has been impaired.

All these men knew that Inspector Strong was not qualified to be commissioner. They knew some sinister force was spreading its tentacles over the city, and they suspected that that force overshadowed police headquarters itself. They were fearful to do positive things, for they could expect no backing from their superiors. Therefore, in the course of a few hours the law-enforcing agencies of the city had become entirely disrupted, and the great metropolis was ripe for the organization of the Dictator to step in and take charge.

However, the nearly panic-stricken residents of the city might have taken some slight courage had they seen the three men who circulated in widespread sections. Those three men moved about as inconspicuously as possible: Wentworth around the Fourteenth Street section; Ram Singh in upper Manhattan; and Jackson in the downtown area. Wentworth, driving across Fourteenth Street in a Drive-Urself car, consulted a sheet of paper on the seat beside him, and braked to a stop alongside the traffic officer at the corner of Fourteenth Street and Broadway.

The officer had been directing traffic in a listless fashion, not troubling to keep his usually keen eye open for traffic violators. Now, as Wentworth stopped beside him, the officer threw him a quizzical glance. Wentworth smiled, said: "Not giving out many tickets tonight, are you, Officer?"

The man shrugged. "What's the use of giving tickets? There may not even be a judge in the city tomorrow."

"Your name is Blaine, isn't it?" Wentworth asked.

The officer nodded. "That's my name." Then he added suspiciously: "What of it?"

Wentworth was studying him. "You're an honest cop. You don't like the way things are being run today, do you?"

Blaine frowned. "Who the devil might you be?"

Wentworth said softly: "I am a friend of a friend of yours."

He lifted the paper that had lain on the seat beside him. "Your name is on this list. You are one of the men whom our mutual friend trust implicitly on the police force."

The death-chatter filled the station.

Then the twin guns backed.

"And who might that mutual friend be?" Blaine asked, becoming more and more annoyed.

Wentworth leaned out of the car, whispered a name in the cop's ear.

Blaine whistled. "Commissioner Kirk—"

"Don't say the name!" Wentworth snapped. "Enough that you know." He fished in his pocket and produced a letter which he handed to the cop. "Do you know this mutual friend's handwriting if you see it?"

"I do, very well. I still have his signature on the written order promoting me to first grade patrolman. But I saw he was in the insane asylum—"

"Read that!" Wentworth commanded.

Puzzled, Blaine opened the note. It read as follows:

TO ALL MY FRIENDS ON THE POLICE FORCE:

The bearer of this letter is Richard Wentworth, who has rescued me from unjust and forcible detention in an insane asylum where I was confined in order to prevent me from fighting the person who is known as the Dictator. All authority over the Police Department has been stripped from me. But I know that my good friends on the force are still ready to fight with me. To those who are loyal, I beg that you will do as Richard Wentworth asks—without question. It is for the sake of the city, and for the sake of your own wives and children.

The letter was signed in the familiar bold handwriting of Commissioner Stanley Kirkpatrick.

Blaine looked up, and his eyes met those of Wentworth

squarely. "I'll do anything for Commissioner Kirkpatrick. And I've heard of you, too, Mr. Wentworth. If you're working with Mr. Kirkpatrick, then I'm with both of you. What are your orders?"

Wentworth spoke swiftly. "I want you to round up every one of the men on this list who are in your precinct. Get them on their feet if they're working, or at home if they're off duty. Have them arm themselves as best they can. If they can smuggle any submachine guns out of the station houses, let them do so.

"Then report, in twos and threes, at the foot of Forty-second Street near the East River. At the spot where Forty-second Street goes through the tunnel under First Avenue, you will be safe from observation at this hour of the night.

"Commissioner Kirkpatrick will meet you. He has established *sub-rosa* headquarters there—and he's going to organize his own police department in an effort to oust the Dictator!"

"By God!" Blaine exclaimed, "I'm with you, Mr. Wentworth! I'll round up every man on this list. We'll be there."

"Try to make it as soon as possible. There is something important to be done before midnight. I'm making the rounds of the precincts, and lining up the key men whose names Kirkpatrick gave me." He reached out of the car and shook hands solemnly with Blaine. "And may success reward our efforts—for the sake of the city's women and children!"

He drove off quickly, and Blaine waved after him, then deliberately deserted his post, walking swiftly south. In contrast to his lackadaisical attitude before, there was now a sparkle in his eye, and a brave lift to his shoulders. He, like thousands of other honest patrolmen, was glad of an opportunity to risk his life in the service of the city.

IN THE basement of the old Hamlin Printing House building under the shadow of the Queensborough Bridge, the hooded man and Olga Laminoff stood alongside the huge water-wheel. Facing him, with their hands bound behind them, were Nita Van Sloan and Elaine Robillard. Each of them had her arms gripped tightly by two men who held them upright.

Nita Van Sloan raised her chin, drew herself up, and shook off the hands of her captors. Her brave eyes met squarely the small, glittering black eyes behind the hood of the Dictator. Olga Laminoff watched Nita Van Sloan keenly, sharply, almost jealously, as if she were envious of the younger woman's courage and bravery.

The Dictator was talking in that quick, eagerly cruel voice of his which reminded Nita so much of a predatory eagle's scream.

"You will notice, Miss Van Sloan, that this turbine wheel rests in a pool of water. Observe how it is turned.

"I suggest that you talk first rather than wait until we have you on the wheel. I merely want to know where your friend, Richard Wentworth, is hiding. Manifestly, he must have a room or some other retreat somewhere in the city. You, as his closest friend, must know where it is. That is all I want you to tell me. We will do the rest."

Nita returned his stare bravely. "I do not choose to talk," she said with a wry smile, paraphrasing a statement of an ex-President of the United States.

The Dictator's hooded head nodded. "I thought you would

be stubborn." A sigh emanated from the hood. "We are forced to proceed."

Just at that moment, a man appeared on the staircase leading from the upper floor. This man was stocky, fat-jowled, with small, frightened eyes. Nita Van Sloan recognized him at once. He was Argyle Dunning, Frank Dunning's uncle, lately the President of the Board of Aldermen, and now Mayor. That he had been admitted thus without ceremony or introduction could indicate only one thing—that he was high in the councils of the Dictator.

The hooded man turned to Argyle Dunning, spoke impatiently: "You're early, Dunning. I thought I told you to come later."

Argyle Dunning glanced around the room, saw Nita and Elaine, and then his eyes rested on the water-wheel. "W-what is that?" he demanded hoarsely.

The Dictator chuckled. "This is an old Chinese custom which we have transplanted to this country. We are about to try to induce Miss Van Sloan here to give us some information. You may stay. You will be entertained."

"Look here," Dunning exclaimed hysterically, pushing forward toward the Dictator. "I won't stand for any more of this. You made a tool of me. I never guessed what you intended to do. When you told me you'd make me Mayor, I didn't know you were going to kill Larrabie in order to do it. I thought you'd get me into the city hall by controlling votes in some manner. Instead you committed murder—*murder, you hear!* And then the killing of Howard Appleton—you framed my own nephew for it, and I dare not even see him or his sweetheart, Evelyn, for fear that they will surmise just by looking at me that I have something to do with it. I tell you, Dictator, I won't go on with this—"

"You object to my methods?" the hooded man asked silkily.

"God help me," Argyle Dunning moaned. "I've made a murderer out of myself." His eyes flashed with sudden hate as they rested on Olga Laminoff. "Because I thought I loved you, I have been a fool—and worse. At first you only asked me to do little things, and I yielded to your charms. Then I became more and more enmeshed, until it was too late to back out. Now you've led me all the way down the road of crime. Now you ask me to stand by and watch while you torture an innocent woman—"

The Dictator broke in coldly. "Dunning, you are a valuable man to me. As Mayor, you are the means by which I control the city. But do not assume that you are absolutely necessary to me. Just as I made you Chief Executive of this city, I can unmake you, and place another in your stead. You *must* go on under my orders."

Argyle Dunning drew himself up to his full height. "There is always the alternative of death, Dictator. My self-respect and my honor are gone. But I can make some sort of amends to society!"

His hand thrust into his jacket pocket, and came out with a small pistol. He covered the Dictator and Olga Laminoff with the gun, and stepped backward, pointing with a shaking finger.

"Release Miss Van Sloan at once, and let her come with me—and the little girl, too!"

The Dictator did not seem particularly frightened by Dunning's pistol. He seemed to hesitate a moment, then his hooded head turned toward Nita and Elaine, and he said airily:

"It's too bad that we must lose your company, Miss Van Sloan. Mr. Dunning wants you to go with him."

Just then there was a quick, loud report. Argyle Dunning uttered a short scream, and a black hole appeared in the side of his head just above the temple.

Dunning in his excitement had forgotten the other thugs in the room. They had been in the shadow, near the double doors leading to the pier, and he had made the mistake of not watching them. Now, one of them had fired from his coat pocket.

Dunning's mouth fell open, and his eyes became vacant. For a moment his body teetered on wobbly knees, then he crashed to the floor, lay there inert, unmoving.

The executioner sighed, and moved back to his position at the wheel. The thug who had shot Dunning snickered. But the Dictator growled at him: "You fool! Couldn't you have shot him in the arm instead of killing him? I needed Dunning. Now I have to go to all the trouble of finding myself another mayor to take his place!"

Suddenly, as if seeking some other place to vent his anger, he swung on Nita. "Now, Miss Van Sloan, we can proceed."

He motioned peremptorily to two of his men, and they seized her, dragged her toward the wheel.

They swung her up onto the wheel, and in spite of her kicking and struggling, they lashed her tightly to it, on her back, with her head down.

Then they stepped back, and the Dictator approached her. The blood was rushing to Nita's head, and the hooded figure, seen upside-down that way, seemed to be dancing before her eyes. She bit her lip, said with an effort at steadiness: "Perhaps, before I die, you'll tell me who you are. Being only a woman, I hate to die with my curiosity unsatisfied."

The Dictator chuckled. "You are a very brave young woman. But your curiosity must remain unsatisfied, as is the curiosity of everybody else. I will tell you, though, that the face behind this hood is the face of a man who is known to many people in this city—yet there is not a single person living in this world who can say that it is the face of the Dictator—not even Olga Laminoff."

Olga Laminoff stepped forward. "But I knew you—"

"Yes, indeed, my dear Olga. You knew me in the old days. But my face was not one that could venture with impunity through the streets of any civilized city. Therefore, I have had it changed. It is that changed face which is known to the people of New York. You, my dear Olga, have never seen it."

Nita Van Sloan spoke desperately, striving for time. "Surely, you can lose nothing by showing your face to me. If I am to die.…"

The hooded man shook his head. "I regret that it is impossible, Miss Van Sloan. We will now proceed."

Nita shut her eyes as the executioner slowly turned the wheel, and her head approached the water beneath.…

CHAPTER 11
BENEATH THE HOOD

UNDER THE First Avenue ramp at Forty-second Street, a mass of blue-coated men stood closely packed in the darkness, listening to the voice of Commissioner Kirkpatrick as he stood on a soap box, towering commandingly over them.

"You men," he was saying, "are those in the Department whom I know to be honest, trustworthy, and imbued with a spirit of civic pride. You have all seen the Police Department debauched. You have seen the city thrown into chaos by the organization of this Dictator who has appeared to grasp power without opposition."

Kirkpatrick glanced at his watch. "It is close to midnight. We were late in getting together, and now we must hurry. You know what you all are to do. Two hundred men on the Forty-second Street side, a hundred on the Vanderbilt Avenue side, the other three hundred of you to be spread out to cover all the other exits of the station. We must not get there before midnight, or our plans will be given away. We must time our arrival so as to catch all of the Dictator's men within the station—that is, of course, assuming that they will be within the station.

"Now one more word before we start—I have learned authoritatively that the person who is known as the Spider is going to try to help us at Grand Central Station. He is there now. I know that the Spider has worked outside the law, and is wanted by the law. But in this emergency we must forget that. I ask you, men, not to attack the Spider tonight if you see him. And I ask you also, to permit him to leave unmolested if we should be successful."

There was a moment's silence, then Kirkpatrick raised his hand. "Let's go!"

He leaped off the soap box, and started the march across Forty-second Street to Grand Central Station.

At one minute before midnight, the vast expanse of Grand Central Station seemed to be more crowded than usual. Trains were leaving in two and three sections to accommodate the great exodus of residents who were fleeing from the impending anarchy which they expected to take possession of the city.

All these people, hurrying with their bags to make late trains, were nervously aware of the fact that there were no police in evidence. Their panic might have been increased tenfold had they noticed the numerous sharp-faced, hard-eyed men who slouched around at many spots in the station, carrying large, awkward bundles under their arms. To the casual eye these men might also have been travelers waiting for their train. But to the eye of Richard Wentworth as he made his way across the station, those men were the shock troops of the Dictator's organization.

His glance, swiftly traveling over the crowd, spied Martin Kreamer standing at the entrance to the waiting room. Behind Martin Kreamer he glimpsed Ram Singh and Jackson, whom he had instructed to wait outside of the main room.

Wentworth saw a dozen or so uniformed men across the station toward the cashier's windows. These were the armed guards from the money wagon which came every night at midnight to remove the day's receipts to the main office of the railroad. These men were marching two by two, each pair carrying a money box.

With a great air of casualness, Wentworth passed several of the lounging men, appearing to pay them no attention. He proceeded to the elevator bank, and took an elevator to the first floor. The tall office building above the Grand Central Station was open all night, but the mezzanine balcony which overlooked the main floor of the station was generally closed after eight o'clock. Wentworth found the hall stair, and descended the half flight to the balcony. The door was locked, but Wentworth withdrew a bunch of keys from his pocket, tried three, and on the last try succeeded in getting the door open. He slipped in quickly, closed the door behind him, and made his way along the darkened balcony toward the railing.

Swiftly, Wentworth removed from under his coat the cape and hat which were so well known to the city as the apparel of the Spider. He donned these, and quickly inserted the false teeth, applied the plastic material to his face which transformed him into the ugly being that was known as the Spider. Now he stepped to the rail and leaned against it, virtually unseen in the darkness up here.

Now his glance focused on the door of the Chief Cashier's booth, and he saw the armed guards begin to come out, each pair carrying a loaded money-box between them. It was quite apparent that the boxes were much heavier than they had been on the way in, for the shoulders of the guards sagged with their weight. And abruptly a strange tenseness seemed suddenly to have descended upon the whole station.

Wentworth was watching Martin Kreamer. The Five-Star Detective Agency head took a small object from his pocket, placed it to his lips. That object was a whistle. He blew a single blast, and the atmosphere of poised tenseness dissolved into one blinding, deadly action. Wrappers were torn from those awkward-looking packages, and the vicious snouts of submachine guns appeared.

Women screamed at sight of the weapons. Wentworth glanced anxiously at the entrances of the station, looking in vain for the appearance of the bluecoats under Kirkpatrick. They were late. He alone, with Ram Singh and Jackson as his only support, must combat this menace.

The armed guards had stopped stock still at sight of those machine guns. And abruptly, without any warning whatsoever, those shifty-eyed thugs began to pull the trips of their machine guns, spraying lead in a deadly hail across the bodies of the guards. Others of the thugs swung their machine guns, indiscriminately spouting fire and lead at the innocent bystanders. Men and women screamed, turned and ran in wild panic in every direction. The marching hail of slugs caught many of them in mid-stride, flung them to the floor, riddled in a dozen places.

And into all that chaos of battle and sudden death, there came the twin screams of deadly slugs from the two guns of the Spider up in the balcony above. Wentworth had thrown himself into the fray. It was not thus that he had planned. He had merely stationed himself here for the purpose of spotting the hooded Dictator, should he be present. He had counted on the police to be here before the stroke of midnight. For some reason they were late.

From the doorway of the waiting room, Ram Singh and Jackson swung into action in a flank attack on the gunmen. The three of them shot coolly, steadily, methodically, making each shot

152

count. Gunner after gunner among the thugs fell under their accurate marksmanship. But there were too many of them. The sights of machine guns were suddenly raised toward the balcony, where the Spider's dark shape was discernible in the shadows.

Martin Kreamer, standing near the ticket window, shouted excitedly: "That's the Spider! Get the Spider!"

Wentworth's magazines were empty. He crouched behind the railing, and his swift fingers slipped new clips into the automatics. Then, raising his head once more, he resumed firing. Those thugs down there were shooting quickly, hurriedly, in their hasty panic. They were anxious—desperately anxious—to get the Spider before the Spider got them. Ram Singh and Jackson had also reloaded, and one or two of the thugs were swinging their submachine guns toward where the two servants stood in the waiting room. Wentworth shot those two before he fired at the ones who were aiming at himself.

Wentworth saw, out of the corner of his eye, that Kreamer had run forward toward the balcony, and was now raising his gun, sighting carefully upward. The Spider snapped a shot at Kreamer, and the Five-Star Detective Agency head was smashed backward as if a giant hand had thrust against his chest. Now a steady hail of slugs was driving Wentworth back from the railing. He crouched, ran along the balcony for ten or fifteen feet, then raised his head again and began to fire from the new point of vantage. Down below, the thunderous explosions, the acrid smell of cordite and the screams of frightened and dying men and women filled the station, made it a scene of bedlam. These people had been betrayed. The police protection that they had a right to expect was not there.

Above them, one man, a man proscribed by the law, was fighting for them. Down below, two servants of that same man were also fighting for them.

Desperately the Spider glanced at the clock. It was three minutes after twelve. Three minutes was a long time for a battle like that to last. Where were the police—

Suddenly he had his answer. Through every entrance there came marching the orderly ranks of blue-coated patrolmen. Commissioner Kirkpatrick strode at the head of those who had come through the Forty-second Street entrance. In the leading ranks of each group of patrolmen were those who were armed with submachine guns; and these sprayed the crowd of gunmen grimly, mercilessly. Behind the policemen with the submachine guns came uniformed men with revolvers—men who had been awarded medals for marksmanship, who had learned how to shoot in the hardest school in the world—the Police Academy.

And those thugs, who had been so brave in cutting down defenseless men and women, lost their nerve before the steady advance of the blue-coated policemen. They fired a few shots, then drew down their guns and raced madly for the opposite entrance of the station.

In a moment the organized attack of these gunmen was changed into a panic-stricken rout. The gunmen fled in every direction, stopped at each entrance by the blue wall of uniformed men. And these criminals were suddenly gripped with the white fear of death. They saw no mercy in the grim eyes of the men of the law; nevertheless, they threw down their guns and raised their hands in the air, and begged for mercy.

While the work of segregating the thugs and carrying out the wounded was going on, a dark apparition appeared on the stairway leading from the balcony. Several of the patrolmen saw that familiar, caped figure, and their hands streaked once more to their holsters. Then they remembered Commissioner Kirkpatrick's orders, and stood silent, watching the Spider cross the floor toward the Commissioner. He reached Kirkpatrick, and the Commissioner glanced around, saw that no one was within earshot of them, and said swiftly: "You've got to cover me, Dick. I told these boys not to molest you, but it would be better if I didn't appear too friendly to you."

"Right, Kirk," Wentworth whispered. Then he raised his voice, spoke so that his tones carried across the whole room: "Commissioner Kirkpatrick, the Spider has helped you here. Do not try to detain me."

Kirkpatrick repressed a grin, and said formally: "Spider, I am compelled to place you under arrest—"

In a flash, the Spider's automatics appeared once more in his hands. "Don't move," he warned everybody, "or I'll shoot the Commissioner!"

It might have been easy for some of the patrolmen in the room to have thrown a quick shot at Wentworth in the hope of killing him before he shot Kirkpatrick. But these men knew that the Spider had just helped to fight their battle for them. Perhaps they felt a sneaking admiration for the Spider. In any event, no shot was fired. Slowly, the Spider marched Kirkpatrick across the station toward the doorway. He caught a glimpse of Ram Singh and Jackson, and jerked his head in their direction. They came swiftly toward them, and when they approached, Wentworth said urgently: "Ram Singh! You followed the Laminoff woman from the Tombs? You saw where she went before going to Grogan's place?"

Ram Singh nodded. "Yes, *sahib*. She went to an old printing house near Fifty-ninth Street. She stayed there only a short time, then went to Grogan's." He had spoken very low, so that none of those in the station heard him.

The eyes of the Spider were flashing behind his disguise. "Ram Singh," he said in a loud voice, "if you will go to the old printing house on the East River near Fifty-ninth Street, you will find your master, Richard Wentworth, awaiting you. And you, Kirkpatrick, will have a good chance of catching the Dictator. This is a tip from the Spider!"

THE EYES of little Elaine Robillard were red from weeping. She was on her knees on the cold basement floor of the Hamlin Printing Concern Building, biting her lips so that the blood came from them. With her hands tied behind her back, it was impossible for her to wipe from her face the tears that coursed freely down her cheeks.

In the center of the room the huge turbine wheel was slowly turning, with Nita Van Sloan tied to it. Nita's head was less than six inches from the water. Her hair, dripping, and hanging from her head, was just touching the water. It was the twentieth time that she had been immersed up to her neck. Each time they had left her in for only a second, then the huge wheel had turned back, dragging her up.

Now, as she was being once more lowered, she was drawing in great, tortured gusts of breath, steeling herself against the next ordeal.

The half dozen of the Dictator's thugs in the room were standing at the far end near the broad open doors which gave egress to the river. Several power boats were tied up here, riding without lights. The crews of those boats, a half dozen in number, had clambered up on the pier which jutted out from the building, and were watching the scene with eager enthusiasm.

Abruptly, with startling suddenness, a single shot sounded from somewhere outside the building.

The Dictator started, and raised his hooded head. Almost at once, there were other shots, then a veritable fusillade sounded from above. The crackling of machine guns mingled with the duller reverberations of heavy police pistols.

The Dictator motioned to his waiting thugs, and started to run toward the staircase. From above there came another sound—the sound of exploding dynamite.

The Dictator cried out: "They've dynamited the doors. We're being attacked!"

The firing upstairs became louder now, as the fighting moved inside the house.

The Dictator backed away from the stairs, motioned to his gunmen to go up. They started forward, but recoiled as the figure of a man appeared on the stairs above them.

Nita Van Sloan could not see this man, but little Elaine

Robillard saw him. She uttered a glad little cry: "Mr. Wentworth! Come and send these bad men away!"

Wentworth had shed the disguise of the Spider, and had hurried to join the police here. Now he came down those stairs like a thunderbolt. In either hand his automatics were blazing death at the gunmen. They retreated swiftly, firing over their shoulders as they ran toward the boats tied up at the pier. Behind Wentworth, Commissioner Kirkpatrick, Ram Singh and Jackson launched themselves down those stairs, guns spitting death, with a stream of bluecoats swarming after them.

The hooded Dictator leaped backward and he put the huge wheel between himself and the attackers. Viciously, he reached over and swung the wheel down so that Nita's head was thrust deep below the water. Then the hooded man dashed for the open doorway leading to the pier.

Now he was in the open, and Wentworth raised his gun, grimly aiming for the man's head.

At that moment little Elaine Robillard screamed: "You wicked man! I hate you!" She stumbled to her feet and threw herself bodily at the Dictator, directly in the line of Wentworth's fire. The Spider eased the pressure on the trigger of his gun.

And in that second the Dictator seized Elaine by the arm, ran, dragging her as a shield, toward the pier.

Elaine struggled, kicking at him, and the Dictator swung at her viciously, still running. Elaine's foot caught in the Dictator's legs, and he tripped headlong, letting go of the child.

But as he fell, the hood dropped from his head.

A shout went up from Ram Singh and Jackson. The man's

face was revealed in the light. And there, staring at them with intense hate written across his gross features, was the battered, square countenance of—Casey Grogan, the ex-pugilist!

Casey Grogan, the man who had cloaked his bid for power under the disguise of the proprietor of a cheap dance hall!

IT WAS thus that the Dictator had fooled the public. Throwing suspicion in turn upon Argyle Dunning, upon Hugh Varner, upon Stephen Pelton, he had himself trod the streets of the city with immunity, sheltered under the grotesque face of a battered prizefighter. Count Calypsa had once been a handsome man. He had reversed the usual process of facial surgery—instead of changing his face to a more handsome one, he had changed it to an uglier one. No one would have suspected that a man would deliberately change his face to assume the appearance of a punch-drunk ex-prizefighter.

Now the Dictator, unmasked, leaped to his feet and raced through the open door to the pier, while the police sent a fusillade of bullets after him.

Richard Wentworth did not fire. Neither did Ram Singh or Jackson. For all three had seen Nita's body tied to the wheel, and they had all rushed to pull her out.

Wentworth untied her, and applied first aid. Nita choked and gasped. She had not lost consciousness, for the entire time of her immersion had been less than three-quarters of a minute. In so short a time had the fortunes of the Dictator changed. From the master of the underworld of a great city he had suddenly become a hunted criminal.

The police under Kirkpatrick dashed out on the pier, sent

their shots flashing into the night at the motor boat which sped away into the river. It was hopeless to pursue that man. He had escaped.

Kirkpatrick shrugged and turned back into the room. Swiftly he issued orders to his men.

"Down to Headquarters, boys. Place Inspector Strong under arrest as being an accessory to Casey Grogan, alias the Dictator. Take charge of all departments, and wait for my arrival!"

Now he turned to Wentworth, who was supporting Nita. Ram Singh had untied little Elaine Robillard, and had had a good deal of trouble identifying himself without his beard.

Now Wentworth, with his arm close around Nita's waist, looked somberly at Kirkpatrick. There was an unspoken question in his eyes.

Kirkpatrick nodded. "Yes, Dick, he got away." The Commissioner's eyes traveled across the floor, over the bodies of dead gunmen, to rest upon the cold, twisted corpse of the beautiful woman, Olga Laminoff. A deep red stain covered her breast. She had been shot in the early minutes of the battle. Whether the bullet which had killed her had been fired from the gun of one of the Dictator's thugs, or of one of the police, was not yet known. But in death, there was still written upon her face the cold beauty which must have intrigued the ruthless Count Calypsa.

"I wonder," Kirkpatrick said softly, "if we'll ever hear from him again."

Wentworth, clasping Nita close to him, looked across her head at Kirkpatrick and laughed harshly. "I'm afraid we will,

Kirk. That man isn't through yet. Did you see the printing presses upstairs? The Dictator must have printed millions of dollars of counterfeit money. That money is probably out now, and will flood the country. He'll have resources—great resources. Yes, Kirk, I'm afraid we're not through with Count Calypsa!"

Nita Van Sloan snuggled closer into Wentworth's arms. "Dick! Then—what about our world cruise?"

He smiled tightly. "It'll have to wait, darling. The city has to be cleaned up. Kirk will need our help. We've got to wipe out the last remnants of the Dictator's organization. We've got to prepare to meet his next blow."

"What about Hugh Varner?" Kirkpatrick asked. "You told me that you had traced a telephone number to him—"

Wentworth nodded. "It was a blind. Calypsa had ordered a telephone installed in the Electrical Building, in Hugh Varner's name, without Varner's knowledge. Then he had caused the wire to be tapped into his own telephone. When Varner's number was dialed, the telephone in his own office rang, and if the number were traced, it would be credited to Varner."

Little Elaine Robillard tugged at Wentworth's sleeve. "Mr. Wentworth! Take me away from here—from all these dead men. I want to go home!"

With a low cry, Nita reached over and drew the little girl close to her breast. "My little sweetheart," she said softly. "From now on I'm going to make sure that you're never dragged into anything like this. I'll take you away with me—far away from this city!"

"Amen to that!" Richard Wentworth said in a deep-throated voice.

Ram Singh nodded in approval. "It will be better fighting, with all due respect to the *memsahib*, when there are no women to worry about." His white teeth flashed in a smile. "When this evil count returns, we will have a royal welcome for him!"

Nita and Wentworth were looking deeply into each other's eyes. Wentworth knew what it meant for her to go away when there was the prospect of more danger and excitement and thrill. But in his heart he was glad. Because he knew that when Calypsa returned, there would be no mercy in the heart of that man for anyone whom Richard Wentworth loved....

POPULAR HERO PULPS AVAILABLE NOW:

THE SPIDER
- ❏ #1: The Spider Strikes — $13.95
- ❏ #2: The Wheel of Death — $13.95
- ❏ #3: Wings of the Black Death — $13.95
- ❏ #4: City of Flaming Shadows — $13.95
- ❏ #5: Empire of Doom! — $13.95
- ❏ #6: Citadel of Hell — $13.95
- ❏ #7: The Serpent of Destruction — $13.95
- ❏ #8: The Mad Horde — $13.95
- ❏ #9: Satan's Death Blast — $13.95
- ❏ #10: The Corpse Cargo — $13.95
- ❏ #11: Prince of the Red Looters — $13.95
- ❏ #12: Reign of the Silver Terror — $13.95
- ❏ #13: Builders of the Dark Empire — $13.95
- ❏ #14: Death's Crimson Juggernaut — $13.95
- ❏ #15: The Red Death Rain — $13.95
- ❏ #16: The City Destroyer — $13.95
- ❏ #17: The Pain Emperor — $13.95
- ❏ #18: The Flame Master — $13.95
- ❏ #19: Slaves of the Crime Master — $13.95
- ❏ #20: Reign of the Death Fiddler — $13.95
- ❏ #21: Hordes of the Red Butcher — $13.95
- ❏ #22: Dragon Lord of the Underworld — $13.95
- ❏ #23: Master of the Death-Madness — $13.95
- ❏ #24: King of the Red Killers — $13.95
- ❏ #25: Overlord of the Damned — $13.95
- ❏ #26: Death Reign of the Vampire King — $13.95
- ❏ #27: Emperor of the Yellow Death — $13.95
- ❏ #28: The Mayor of Hell — $13.95
- ❏ #29: Slaves of the Murder Syndicate — $13.95
- ❏ #30: Green Globes of Death — $13.95
- ❏ #31: The Cholera King — $13.95
- ❏ #32: Slaves of the Dragon — $13.95
- ❏ #33: Legions of Madness — $12.95
- ❏ #34: Laboratory of the Damned — $12.95
- ❏ #35: Satan's Sightless Legion — $12.95
- ❏ #36: The Coming of the Terror — $12.95
- ❏ #37: The Devil's Death-Dwarfs — $12.95
- ❏ #38: City of Dreadful Night — $12.95
- ❏ #39: Reign of the Snake Men — $12.95
- ❏ *NEW:* #40: Dictator of the Damned — $12.95

THE WESTERN RAIDER
- ❏ #1: Guns of the Damned — $13.95
- ❏ #2: The Hawk Rides Back from Death — $13.95
- ❏ *NEW:* #3: Gun-Call for the Lost Legion — $13.95

G-8 AND HIS BATTLE ACES
- ❏ #1: The Bat Staffel — $13.95

CAPTAIN SATAN
- ❏ #1: The Mask of the Damned — $13.95
- ❏ #2: Parole for the Dead — $13.95
- ❏ #3: The Dead Man Express — $13.95
- ❏ #4: A Ghost Rides the Dawn — $13.95
- ❏ #5: The Ambassador From Hell — $13.95

DR. YEN SIN
- ❏ #1: Mystery of the Dragon's Shadow — $12.95
- ❏ #2: Mystery of the Golden Skull — $12.95
- ❏ #3: Mystery of the Singing Mummies — $12.95

CAPTAIN ZERO
- ❏ #1: City of Deadly Sleep — $13.95
- ❏ #2: The Mark of Zero! — $13.95
- ❏ #3: The Golden Murder Syndicate — $13.95